LUNA CAPTURED

LUNA RISING
BOOK TWO

SARA SNOW

CHAPTER ONE
RUBY

Have you ever been so hungry that your stomach feels like it's caving in on itself? So thirsty you can barely pry your tongue from the roof of your mouth? Your mind focuses on nothing but food and drink, drink and food. How a stale piece of bread, a glass of water, or a single French fry might save your life.

If you've never felt that, you're lucky, and I hope you never do. I wasn't suffering from hunger only. My hair was matted to my skull, and I was getting sick of my own foul odor. I'd lost track of how long I'd been chained up in Axel's dungeon, and I was passing out more frequently due to hunger and dehydration.

My eyes cracked open as I listened to the dripping water coming from somewhere inside this dark dungeon. It was making this situation a hundred times worse. Every time I heard it, I thought about how even one tiny drop in my mouth might make this situation a little more bearable.

My tongue felt like sandpaper, and my back felt sore from lying down for so long. I, however, didn't have the strength to turn onto my side. My eyes started to sting with what should have been tears, and I lifted a shaky hand to brush them away. But no tears came. My body had none to spare....

My hand fell to my side as my body was wracked with sobs.

This is what my life has come to. Over the years I've endured my share of horrible hardship but this, this takes the cake. I had finally accomplished my dream of getting into college and now, less than two months later, I've been abducted by a werewolf with a vendetta. Yes, werewolves are real. I had the rotten luck of being mated to not just one, but two werewolves. One hates me, and the other was just starting to warm up to me before I was taken away from him.

Axel has locked me in a dungeon, while Xavier had convinced his father to let me live with him and his pack. Where Xavier is sweet, quiet, and calm, Axel is crude and cruel. They are polar opposites, as apparently are their dueling packs. Whoever their goddess is that has done this to me, I need to have a talk with her. I had wasted time thinking Axel would reject me because I'm not a wolf, never realizing he had other plans until it was too late.

I sighed and found the strength to roll unto my side. The chain on my ankle felt much heavier than it had earlier since my strength was quickly diminishing, and it took a few tries before I was able to move my leg.

Axel's threat that he was going to use me to get rid of Xavier's pack replayed in my mind yet again, and my dehydrated body managed to spare a tear. I had no idea how he planned on using me to accomplish that, but whatever his plan was, he would fail. I was pretty sure he would fail, anyways. Mathieu and Xavier's pack didn't seem like they would be easy to take down.

Why do I have to be the first human to be mated to a werewolf? And two at once? This is all new to me, and them as well. Even if Xavier were to find me and free me from Axel's chains, I would still have to worry about the fact that the Werewolf Council, their governing body, is after me as well.

There won't be an end to this unless I die. That's becoming clear.

My life has been nothing but a series of unfortunate events since I was a child. I'm tired of it all. Weeks ago I was a normal college girl trying to get through life with a bright future ahead of her, and now I am wasting away in a dungeon waiting to see how I will die (and at whose hands). That's just the kind of shit that would happen only to me.

The door to the dungeon opened. With my back turned, I didn't bother to look around. Whoever it was, they would leave eventually if I pretended to be asleep. My heartbeat accelerated when I heard keys jiggling in the lock to my cell and then, rusted hinges screeching.

Someone was coming into my cell, and whomever it was could most definitely hear my heartbeat. I remained still, now frozen with fear when I heard footsteps approach me. A warm hand grabbed me by my hair.

"Get off me!" I screamed.

I was yanked onto my feet, and then thrown back down onto the small bed. I looked up into Axel's hazel eyes as I sunk my teeth into my lips. Natalie, the only wolf that has been kind to me from the start, had told me mates can't hurt each other. Clearly, that had been bullshit.

He bent down and began to remove the chain from around my ankle before rising to his towering height again. My heart was pounding, my eyes wide as I watched him. He didn't speak. He didn't even look at me before throwing the chain to the side and grabbing my arm.

"You're hurting me! What are you doing?"

His tight hold on my arm would leave a bruise, but I was too scared to care. He was dragging me out of the cell and outside, my weak legs struggling to keep up with him. Fresh air filled my lungs, and my eyes closed for a second before I was yanked forward to keep up with him.

"Where are you taking me?" He didn't answer. "Axel, where are you taking me? Please, you're hurting me!"

I channeled what little strength I had left into pulling away from him. He released me, but within seconds he grabbed me by the hair. Fire blossomed at my scalp, my hair felt like it was going to be ripped out, and I clenched my teeth to stop myself from screaming. My eyes grew teary as I reached up to hold his hand, and I felt him loosen his hold. I could barely see his face, but his eyes were like headlights.

He continued walking, and I dug my heels into the ground to not move and started screaming. If he was going to kill me, I wasn't going to die quietly. Oh, hell, no! I didn't ask to be mated to him, and if I could change that, I would in a heartbeat. I've done nothing to deserve being treated like this.

He released my hair to grab my chin, his fingers digging into my cheeks, but not painfully so. It was as if he had forgotten just how strong he was at first, but was now being cautious. I knew if he wanted to, he only had to squeeze a little and my jaw would break.

His face dipped to mine. I was able to see him clear enough and quickly fell silent. The color in his eyes vanished, replaced by blackness as they transformed into that of his wolf.

"Be quiet, or I'm going to rip your tongue out."

I said nothing as I stared up at him. We stood in silence. No doubt he was waiting to see if I'd speak, and when I didn't, he released my face and grabbed my arm. He continued dragging me through the woods, twigs, and stones poking and piercing into my feet as I silently followed him.

I felt like I could no longer ask if he would hurt me or not. That wasn't a chance I wanted to take. Suddenly, I tripped and almost fell. His hold on my arm quickly tightened, and he pulled me up. He didn't stop and continued pulling me before I properly had my footing again.

The woods around us were thick, even thicker than where

Xavier lived, and I almost collided into him as he suddenly stopped. I was panting as if I had been running for a mile when a man appeared from behind a tree, his body cloaked in darkness. I squinted to see his face, but I could only make out an outline. Soon I gave up, deciding instead to focus on catching my breath.

"That's a human," the man said and I stopped breathing. "Why is there a human here?"

"That is none of your business. Continue with your patrol and tell no one about seeing her. Do I make myself clear?"

Axel walked away before the man could respond, and I kept my head down as my legs worked to keep by his side. I felt like gravity was pulling me down further and further as my body began to feel heavy. I was exhausted, my legs now putty.

Lights from a house appeared through the trees ahead and I swallowed, a million scenarios of what was about to happen running through my mind. I had assumed Axel's little dungeon had to be on his pack's land but now he was taking me to what looks like his house. I was terrified but I was too tired, too burned out to care. All I needed was a glass of water, nothing else.

I collapsed, my body shutting down finally, and Axel grabbed me before I could hit the ground. He shook me violently, and I was rattled awake.

"Don't you fucking fall asleep. I'm not carrying you."

"Water," I whispered, and he pulled me back onto my feet.

He wrapped his arm around my waist instead, and we made our way inside the house. I had no idea when we had even left the woods to approach the house, but here we were. Bright lights burned my eyes as we entered the house. I squinted my eyes as he continued dragging me, cool tile now beneath my feet.

If he was going to kill me, now was the best time. I was too tired to feel anything. But when he pulled open a door and we descended a flight of stairs into pitch-black darkness, I started to panic. Had he taken me from one cage to put me into another? No, no, I wasn't doing that again.

"Axel, no, let go!"

He threw me to the ground, and a light turned on. We were in a basement, but it looked like it had recently been cleaned out. There was a bed, a table and chair, and nothing else, but it was so much better than being locked up in that cold dark cell.

I got onto my knees as he turned to leave, and he casually pointed to a door I hadn't noticed. "Take a bath. You smell horrible."

He closed the door behind him and didn't spare a backward glance. I remained on my knees as my bottom lip began to tremble. Holding my hand out, I looked at the dirt that had built up on my skin and under my nails and fell to my side to lie on the ground. I began to shake, my hand flying to my mouth to silence my sobs.

"I fucking hate you," I said softly before inhaling deeply and sitting upright. "I hate you! You hear me!"

After mustering up what strength I had left, I got up off the ground and walked towards the door he had pointed to. Behind it was a tiny bathroom with clothes already folded onto the closed toilet seat along with a comb. That was all that was provided, and I was grateful for it. I stripped slowly and avoided looking into the small mirror above the sink. I didn't need to know what I looked like. Besides, I knew if I looked, I would end up more broken than I already was.

"Xavier, please come for me." I prayed as I climbed into the tiny shower and pulled the shower curtain. "Please come for me."

I turned the shower on, and ice-cold water shot out to pelt my body. I didn't care how cold it was, I was too happy to see water to complain about the temperature. I drank the water until I couldn't anymore, and as I lathered up my body and hair, I started to cry yet again. Only this time the tears came.

What is it about taking a shower while sad that makes all your emotions bubble to the surface? My tears were washed away with the water, but they kept coming. What was going to happen after this? Why had he moved me? Where is Xavier?

So many questions began to ricochet off the walls in my mind. What was Axel planning? He had said I had provided him with the perfect chance to be rid of the Blackmoon pack. How had I done that?

I watched the dirt and muck wash down the drain and kept scrubbing my body until the water was no longer colored. I shook my head and stepped out of the shower to grab the small towel that was under the clothes on the toilet and began patting my body dry. If I continued like this, I would only stress myself out more than I already was. There was simply no way for me to know what Axel's plan was, and I was only hurting myself further by imagining endless possible scenarios.

I got dressed in the jeans and small black t-shirt that had been provided for me before taking a look in the mirror.

My eyes and cheeks were a little sunken, my collar bones were more prominent, and I could pull the waist of the pants away from my body easily. My hair was still its normal vibrant red, maybe more so now because I was now a lot paler. In conclusion, I looked a mess.

There was a travel-size toothbrush and toothpaste, so of course, I brushed my teeth twice. I felt like I was a new person afterward, and made my way back into the room, my mind set on going to sleep. The cold shower had been enough to force a little energy back into my body. I felt rejuvenated, but yearned for a good night's sleep. Despite having plans to fall into bed and sleep for a decade, my stomach had its own plans as it growled loudly when my eyes fell on a large bowl of fruits on the table.

That hadn't been there before, I said to myself. I took a step towards it before stopping myself. My eyes then wandered to the stairs and door, and I went up the stairs instead.

I knew the odds of it being unlocked were low, but I tried nonetheless. It didn't budge, and even though I had been expecting as much, I still grew angry. Karma was going to take care of Axel for me. Whether I lived or died, such cruelty cannot go unpunished.

I looked down at my arm and sure enough, my skin was bruised from his dragging me through the woods, his fingerprints still visible.

"Let me out!" I screamed. Hoping he could hear me. "You fucking asshole let me out! You can't keep me locked away forever!" I started pounding on the door, anger filling me up with energy. "Let me out dammit! Axel! Reject me then! Coward!"

The door swung open and I staggered backward, almost falling down the stairs as a man filled up the frame of the door almost completely. A single arm was both my arms combined, and if his size wasn't scary enough, he pinned me with his black stare. My body froze as he flashed his fangs at me and growled, and although I tried, I wasn't able to conceal the way I jumped with fear.

He looked me up and down as if I was shit stuck to the bottom of his shoe before grabbing the handle of the door and slamming it shut. Then I heard the low click of the door locking once more, and my bravado and energy disappeared all at once.

"I hope you can hear me, Axel," I said as I went back down the stairs and towards the bed. "I fucking hate you."

CHAPTER TWO
RUBY

I stared at the small window across the room that was too far up the wall for me to try and break through. Sure, I'd be able to reach it if I stood on the table, but what would happen after I got outside? I'd get chased by wolves that I could never outrun. Where would I even run to? I had no idea where I was to begin with. For all I knew, there was no one but wolves for a hundred miles in every direction.

It was morning, but I pulled the covers up to my chin and snuggled further into bed. The small old mattress that had passed for a bed inside my cell hadn't been much. While this wasn't great either, there was nothing for me to do, nowhere for me to go, so why not stay in bed a little longer?

I had eaten all the fruits and was still full, so I was fine for the most part. All I could do now was wait for Axel to make his next appearance.

I turned onto my side, but backed up with a scream on my lips as I came face to face with Natalie. She was lying beside me with her hand under her cheek, her blue eyes piercing into my green ones. I blinked rapidly, unable to believe what I was seeing, and she started to smile. She reached out and moved a strand of my hair out of my face, and happiness blossomed in my chest as her finger brushed against my face. She was really here!

"Hey babe," she said and my eyes widened.

"Natalie, is it you? Is it really you?"

It looked like her. Her icy blue eyes were the same, but her platinum hair was now snow-white, more silver than blonde. I frowned at that but said nothing. He nodded to answer my question, and I moved to hug her but froze. No, I needed to think. This can't be real. How did she get in here? I looked down at my wrist, and the scar that was there from my suicide attempt as a teen was gone.

"This isn't real," I said sadly, and the excitement I had been feeling vanished. "You're in my head again, aren't you?"

She gave me a sad smile, and I sighed before lying down again. "I figured. How are you doing this? Am I going to wake up and find you and Xavier in my room?"

"You're not. I'm sorry, but I know Axel is the one that has you."

"You lied to me, Natalie. You said mates can't hurt each other." I tried not to tear up, but I failed. "Get me out of here! You've told Xavier where I am, haven't you?"

She moved her hair behind her ears and pinched the bridge of her nose. She didn't say anything for a while, and I started to worry. I reached out to her and touched her hand, but she felt so cold that I quickly pulled away. I hadn't touched her the last time she had entered my mind like this. I wasn't sure if cold skin was normal, but I noticed she looked like she was in pain.

"Sorry." She said as she moved her hand away. "I've never done this from such a far distance. Finding you alone has been hard enough. I can't stay with you long, Ruby, but I want you to play along with Axel's game. He'll be coming for you soon to tell you he'll be taking you somewhere. Play along, okay? He's told the Council about you, about what's been happening, and now they'll be coming for Xavier."

"Shit."

She exhaled and began to fade and I sat up quickly. "Wait! You've told Xavier, right? Warn him about Axel and the Council. Axel said he was going to use me to finally get rid of the Blackmoon pack."

"It won't get to that, but yes, I'm heading to Xavier now to warn him. Axel is a fool to think the Council won't turn on him, too. You're his mate as well, no matter how much he denies it. The Council wants total obedience and control, so anyone that steps outside of that always suffers. Mathieu and Xavier broke the law by not killing you. It won't matter to them that you are Xavier's mate. All they will care about is the fact that you are human."

So, in the end, it really will be my fault. I never should have moved here.

I felt like screaming, but she reached out and placed her hand on my cheek. Her hand was freezing, but I closed my eyes and allowed the cold to seep into my skin without moving away.

"I don't know if I'll get to Xavier in time, so I have to go."

By now, I was able to see through her as she faded more and more. Her hand fell away from my face. I didn't want her to go, I didn't want to be left alone, but I knew she had to leave. Xavier was now the one in danger.

"Axel won't hurt you, Ruby. He'll act like he can, but it hurts him even more."

I rolled my eyes.

Tell that to my arm that's still bruised.

"H-how is Xavier? Is he okay? Please tell me before you go. I-I..."

Could I say it? I wanted to tell her to tell him I miss him, but even though we had kissed and had been getting close, there was still so much left for us to say to each other.

"You'll see him soon. You can tell him everything yourself then."

She vanished, and I woke up with a start and took a large

intake of breath. I looked around the room frantically before plopping back down.

Yes, finally some good news.

I rolled onto my side to stare out the window again as I began to smile, a genuine one. It's been so long since I've felt a pinch of happiness or hope. But my smile died quickly because I was now worried for Xavier. With the way Natalie and everyone else has been speaking about this 'Council,' it was clear they were to be feared. Natalie seemed to be on top of it, but I just hoped she would get to him in time.

—————•◦ ◦•—————

Anxiety had me pacing around the room, sitting on the floor, and climbing onto the table to see through the window, which revealed nothing but endless trees. Soon I settled for sitting around the table, my hunger returning. Compared to the torture I had endured up until last night, I could ignore the growls my stomach was making.

I've thought about going to sleep a few times in hopes of Natalie returning, but she had mentioned how hard it was to reach out to me. She needed her strength to get to Xavier, so I resisted my impulse to nap just for the sake of talking to her again.

My fingers drummed on the stained surface of the white table as I wondered if she had warned Xavier yet.

I recalled the night I had been abducted, the bliss that had come before the chaos that is, and a heavy sadness settled on my chest. Xavier and I had laid in the woods in each other's arms. I was starting to feel the bond between us, I think. Just when I began to feel drawn to him, I was ripped away. That night he had told me about their goddess, an entity that created the very first werewolf, who decides on each and every wolf's fate. One who had clearly decided on my fate as well.

As far as I could see, she wasn't doing a very good job,

considering she managed to link three people together that could never possibly work out.

I heard the door open and looked to the stairs to see the giant man from last night leading a woman down the stairs. She was wearing combat boots and had red streaks in her black hair. She nodded to the man, and he turned away to head back upstairs. He left the door open, however, and I stared at the woman expectantly while she looked me up and down with disgust. At this point, I was starting to get immune to those stares. I watched as she crossed her hands over her large bosom and walked forward.

"You don't belong here," she said, and I crossed my arms on the table.

Had Axel sent this woman to scare me or something? He could do a much better job with only a glance. Was she here to remind me how much I don't belong here?

I narrowed my eyes at her, and it clicked. No, she knows exactly who I am, who I am to Axel, and it's clearly killing her.

So, I have another Anna on my hands. Lovely.

"We can both agree on that, at least."

A deep crease appeared between her brows as if she hadn't expected me to answer. "It speaks." She said with a smirk, and I blinked slowly at her, doing my best to force a look of indifference onto my face.

"Can I help you with something? As you can see, I'm quite busy."

She hadn't been expecting that response, either. It clearly struck a nerve, because, within the next second, her light brown eyes turned black.

"You have no idea who you're talking to, human."

"That's because we don't know each other. Trust me, you don't want to know me, either. I have enough shit to deal with right now, so whatever issue you have with me *despite* us having *never* met before will have to be resolved at a later date."

I sat back and crossed my arms as she uncrossed hers. She

hunched her shoulders a bit and her mouth opened to reveal that her fangs had come out to play. Her nails began to descend into claws, and I quickly got up from around the table.

I had nowhere to run, but I sure as hell would defend myself as much as possible. This girl wasn't like Anna–she was worse. Where Anna had been all bark and no bite, it was clear this girl was ready and willing to rip my throat out.

"A weak thing like you can never be a wolf's mate."

She charged at me. and my hand rose to protect my face. I was saved by Axel's thundering voice as it echoed through the room.

"Stop!"

I looked up to find the girl's claws frozen inches away from my face. There was a look of straining on her face, and she slowly lowered her hand and turned around.

Behind her, Axel was standing by the stairs with his hands clenched at his sides. His eyes were narrowed dangerously. His curly black hair, usually kept in a ponytail behind his back, was loose now, and it fell in waves over his shoulders. Even I couldn't deny that he was a handsome man, the kind with an aura of danger that draws women in.

"She doesn't belong here." The girl said through clenched teeth. "This weakling can't be your mate. A strong breeze can knock her over. She can't be your mate. She's not worth..."

Axel stepped forward, and the girl swallowed whatever else she was about to say. "Know your place, wolf. My business is not yours, so I'd suggest you leave before I kill you. You are not allowed in here."

She opened her mouth to speak, and Axel's eyes turned black. He growled at her, the sound filling the space around us, and she quickly bowed her head and backed away. She scurried from the room, and Axel's eyes slid to me when he heard the door close behind her.

He turned his body to face me, and his head tilted to the side. "I don't want you talking to anyone."

"You say that as if I get visitors often enough for me to even have the chance to speak to anyone. I wasn't talking to her. She came in here to throw a tantrum."

"So, you said nothing to her? Not one word?"

Why are we even talking about something so trivial? It's not like I had spilled secrets to her. What we needed to talk about was when the hell he'd be getting me out of here. Natalie had said he'd be taking me somewhere maybe that's why he was here now.

Good timing because a second later I would have been mincemeat.

"No," I responded, and he inhaled before walking forward.

I stood my ground despite my heart hammering, and I tilted my head back to look into his black eyes as they slowly changed back to hazel. His eyes roamed over my face, and I frowned. Being so close to him was definitely something I didn't need. He was a gorgeous man, but there was no way I'd never ever let a handsome face make me forget what an asshole he is.

I looked away, my face twisting as my heart began to race. I wasn't attracted to this prick, I couldn't be. Hell no!

"You need to step back," I said with my head still turned to the side. "There is no reason for you to stand this close to me," I added, and his hand shot out to grab my face.

He wasn't squeezing me tightly, but merely holding my face to turn it back towards him. I grabbed his wrist and tried to move away, but he casually slapped my hand away with his other hand.

"I don't like being lied to." He said the words slowly, his minty breath fanning my face. "Do not lie to me, Ruby. Ever, about anything. Now I don't want you to speak to anyone unless I say so. Do you understand me?" I kept my mouth shut, and let the hatred in my eyes speak for me. "Good girl. We'll be going somewhere soon, and I suggest you be on your best behavior."

I had a million things to say in response, but Natalie's words echoed in my mind. I reminded myself that it was my job to play along with Axel's plan. I settled for pulling my face away, and his hand fell to his side. He didn't move away, and neither did I. He didn't look away, and neither did I. I might be weak in strength, but I would not be cowed by any man, wolf or no wolf. Strength isn't only physical.

I frowned when the corner of his mouth began to lift into a smirk, and he shook his head and stepped back. What the hell was he smirking at? Was this fun for him? I narrowed my eyes at him and realized it was. The punk was messing with me.

"Your fire is cute, Ruby, but you will end up getting hurt because of it. Werewolves like obedience. Disrespect and disobedience aren't tolerated, so remember what I just told you. Speak to no one, and you'll continue breathing."

He turned to leave, and I stared daggers at his back, my nails digging into the palms of my hands. What he didn't know was that I hated being told what to do and being given orders, and it didn't matter who was doing the ordering. That wasn't going to change even if the orders were coming from someone who could rip me to shreds if I were a mere sheet of paper. Trust me, I'd had more than my fair share of consequences as a result of my inability to shut the hell up, even when it was probably in my best interest to do so.

Maybe one day my mouth will get me killed, but at least I'll die standing up for myself.

CHAPTER THREE
XAVIER

I could hear a bird chirping in a tree a few meters away, but it sounded like it was resting on my shoulder. My ears twitched as another bird answered the first one's call, and I tried my best to tune them out. I focused on the wind in the trees instead as I continued to walk along the path in the forest. I was heading to the cliff where Ruby and I had sat and talked so long ago.

No, it wasn't so long ago, I thought as I shook my head. Only a week has passed with her being missing. While it was only a week, it was far too long for comfort. It felt like an eternity.

Natalie has been missing for just as long, and I'm not sure how much longer I can survive not knowing what has happened to either of them. My hands clenched at my sides as my rage began to consume me yet again.

Being without Ruby and not knowing if she was hurt or not was taking its toll. My wolf has been clawing under my skin to the point that I've woken up with my sheets and clothes ripped by my claws and fangs out without my conscious command.

There have been no leads on finding Ruby, and no one has called for ransom or to make any demands. She is just gone, vanished into thin air.

Gone.

I turned off the path and headed into the thicker forest, but I didn't get far. I closed my eyes as the haunting sound of Ruby's scream entered my mind. She had screamed when that wolf had attacked her, and that was the moment when I had realized my mistake. They were after her and her alone. The attack on me was just a diversion carefully designed to separate us, and I had played right into their evil hands.

Now Ruby was God-Knows-Where experiencing God-Knows-What while I waited for some sign, any sign, of where I might find her. I growled low as I unclenched my right hand, and I winced a little as my hand began to shift. My bones broke and shifted, and my fingers elongated while my claws extended. I gritted my teeth as I swung around and swiped my claws at a nearby tree.

The mangled tree tilted to the side as if to fall, but stopped, the trunk in shreds. I closed my eyes as I started to lose control of my shift. My fangs began to elongate and graze against my bottom lip, and I clenched my left fist that hadn't shifted and hunched forward. I exposed my right arm and it began to return to normal, my fingers bending in odd directions as my bones broke and reset.

I opened my eyes as I stood upright once more, and I looked down at my hand before clenching and unclenching my fist. My nails were itching to tear through the flesh of whoever had taken Ruby.

"Send her back to me," I said to the forest, but I was hoping the goddess was listening.

I paused for a moment, a familiar scent licking at my nostrils, and as the scent registered, I spun on my heels to find Natalie standing behind me. I blinked rapidly and took a step towards her before stopping.

Something was different about her.

Her eyes were still ice blue, but her hair was white—snow white. She was just standing there staring at me, but there was rigidness about her as if she was frozen to the spot. There was a distant look in her eyes as if she was seeing through me, and I became on edge. I looked her up and down, trying to see if this was somehow a trick. My stance widened to prepare myself for an attack. Her mouth curved with a smile, and I got a glimpse of the Natalie I had known.

What happened to her?

"Natalie?"

"Your wolf—with Ruby being gone you're losing control," she responded as she pointed a finger at me.

I nodded. "Yes, where have you..."

"I can help," she interjected as she began moving towards me. She had her hands raised to show she posed no threat, no doubt having noticed my defensive stance.

I allowed her to get close to me, but my eyes watched her every move. It felt odd for me to be so cautious with her. Her scent was the same, so I knew it was her, but she looked so different. Something was definitely wrong. Why had she vanished? To get her hair done? That's unlikely because Adolfa was found dead.

She raised her hand and pressed her thumb to my forehead. Instantly, warmth rose within me, and days of feeling on edge vanished as my wolf calmed. I sighed as she pulled away. I looked down at my hand, my claws no longer feeling as if they'd appear at any moment.

"How did you do that?" I asked her, but she merely shrugged and stepped back. "What happened to you, Natalie? What happened with Adolfa?"

At the mention of Adolfa's name, she grimaced. "She transferred all of her power to me."

She turned away, and my eyes widened. "How? I didn't know Enchanteds could do that."

Despite the fact that her back was turned to me, I could see her nod. "I didn't know either. There was a lot I didn't know." She turned to face me. "She showed me where Ruby is as well."

That had my wolf stirring yet again and hope blossomed inside me. "A-Are you serious?" She nodded. I laughed and turned away, my legs pumping as I began to run through the forest to head back to the house. "Where is she? We need to get back to the house."

I felt alive for the first time in days. I've been wandering around either on edge or dragging myself like a zombie, but just that quickly, my energy returned to me full force.

"Xavier, wait!"

I skid to a halt as Natalie's voice echoed through the forest. "What? If you know where she is, I need to tell dad. We have to go get her."

"No, we don't. We can't," she said as she walked towards me, and I frowned in confusion. "She's safe where she is for now. We have more immediate issues to take care of."

I stared at her as if I was looking at someone deranged. How could she expect me to not go searching for Ruby? What else could possibly be more important? I've been losing my mind for days wondering where Ruby is and if she's okay. Not to mention how worried I had been about Nathalie herself.

"Where is she?" I asked her, my face now twisted with anger. "There is nothing more important than finding her, Natalie, and you know that."

She stepped forward, her eyes narrowing, and I blinked in surprise at the dominance that was radiating off her. All wolves radiate some level of dominance, but it gets stronger depending on your bloodline and your rank in the pack. Enchanteds can't transform into actual wolves, so they don't radiate as much dominance as the rest of us do.

The stronger the Enchanted, the stronger their dominance level, but Natalie hadn't been this strong before. What else did Adolfa change?

"She is only safe for now, Xavier. The Council knows about her, so they are coming for you. You broke the law by sparing a human."

"She's my mate, I couldn't kill her!"

"They won't give a fuck! She's human. They won't care that she's your mate. You broke the law, and that is all the reason they need to step in. Then they will focus on how a human can be mated to a wolf. They might even try to bury the entire Bloodmoon Pack to hide this. You know they can! Ruby is safe for the time being, but that is all."

I knew she was right, but I needed to find Ruby. We were just getting close to each other, and having her ripped away from me so suddenly left a large hole in my chest. I felt weak without her, and I wondered if she felt the same. Being human, the mate bond didn't affect her the same way. Was she missing me?

"Who has her? Why did Adolfa even transfer her powers to you?"

Natalie pinched the bridge of her nose as she stepped past me, her white hair blowing in the wind. "Why she did it isn't important right now. What's important is getting back to the house and warning your dad. We have an hour before they arrive. Xavier, we don't have time to waste."

I pulled up at her side, and we walked briskly back to the house. There was a lot she wasn't saying, that was clear, but she was right. If the Council was on their way, then we did have a more pressing issue. However, I couldn't help asking one question. I wanted to know who had the balls to take my mate? Who even knew about her? How could she be safe when she had been attacked and taken?

"Who took her?" I asked her and her shoulders moved up and down as she sighed. "I need to know, Natalie. How do you know she's safe?"

"She's safe because she's with Axel. He's the one that took her from you, and he's the one that reported you to the Council."

I should have known that scumbag had something to do with her abduction! Axel's her mate, too. What he doesn't know is that by reporting her and our mate bond to the Council, he just got her killed, and maybe even himself, too.

CHAPTER FOUR
NATALIE

"Axel's a fool to think the Council won't try to dissect him as well for having a human mate. Whatever judgment falls onto our pack because one of us is mated to a human will happen to him, too" Xavier said.

I watched him as he paced back and forth, his hand on his chin. We were filling Mathieu in on what was happening, and word had been sent to the rest of the pack to stay indoors until their alpha said otherwise.

All that really needed to be said was that the Council would be visiting, and all wolves would scatter without being told to anyway. Everyone avoids contact with the Council as much as they can. No one wants their lives looked into, their privacy invaded and stripped down to nothing. That's what the Council likes to do. They feed on knowledge like rats feed on garbage.

"Axel thinks he's acting in the interest of his pack," I said and Mathieu, who was sitting with his elbows on his knees and his hand over his mouth, looked my way. "But he isn't seeing the bigger picture, so yes, there are multiple holes in his plans. He's one of the few wolves left that trusts the Council. Abducting Ruby might have been the only good thing in his plans."

Xavier gave me the same look as before as if I was crazy. I blinked slowly as I stared back at him to show I wasn't about to change what I had just said. When Adolfa transferred her powers to me, I saw more than I honestly wanted to. There was so much I couldn't say, so much I couldn't tell them.

"How was that the good part of his plan? I need Ruby here, with me. She has to leave with us." He turned to Mathieu, who had yet to speak. "Where can we go?"

"I'm not leaving, we're not leaving," Mathieu finally said as he reclined in his seat. He combed his raven hair backward and cracked his knuckles as he stared off into the distance. I knew, however, that the wheels in his mind were turning.

Mathieu didn't earn his place as one of the most respected alphas without being a patient and calculating man. He was a man of few words, but his actions always spoke volumes.

He looked at Xavier. "There is nowhere to go, Xavier. Wherever we go the Council will find us. If Ruby were here, you would leave with her, but that would still leave me, Natalie, and the rest of the pack to suffer. Not all of us can run." He looked my way. "I assume that's why Axel took her–to stop her from leaving with Xavier?"

I nodded and so did he, having already figured out a part of Axel's plan. I was sure he was close to figuring out the rest. He was right, however. There was nowhere any of us could go that the Council wouldn't find us, and Mathieu would never abandon his pack.

"If we run, Xavier, we incriminate ourselves even more," Mathieu added, his fingers now interlocked on his lap. He looked so calm, so collected in the face of danger, it was admirable but if only he knew the chaos that was coming. "We didn't commit a crime or break a law. One of our most fundamental laws is to protect our female mates, the ones that will carry our children to continue our bloodline. She's a human who's found out about us, yes, but she's also a human who's mated to a wolf. I would say that our law to protect her stands above the one to kill her."

Xavier turned away, his shoulders rising and falling with his deep breaths. "Let's hope the Council sees it that way and aren't blinded by their hatred for humans."

Since I had yet to find my mate, I hadn't understood the turmoil within Xavier for not having Ruby by his side. When I had touched him to calm his wolf, however, I had felt it all.

I had felt his fear, the gut-wrenching panic and anger he wrestled with since her abduction, and the blame he was placing on himself for not protecting her.

Finding one's mate is something many wolves look forward to. Supposedly it is like feeling whole for the first time in your life. But me? I wouldn't mind not finding mine right now. I am terrified of one day feeling the agony Xavier was now experiencing. I was young and had fledgling powers when Mathieu had lost his wife, our Luna, but I had a much higher respect for him since I'd felt Xavier's pain. And Ruby was only missing. Mathieu had survived losing his other half.

"I should kill him," Xavier said under his breath, and his words rang with truth and intention.

"Axel took Ruby to stop you from running off with her. The Council is coming because they want to see for themselves if this is all true if a human is truly mated to a wolf, and to two at that. We can use that to our advantage, Xavier. The Council will try to see if either of you is weakened by her." I crossed my hand over my chest and stepped forward. "They will see her as a weak human, someone that can't feel the bond, someone that shouldn't affect you and Axel. Prove that's not true."

"You talk about tricking the Council as if it's child's play, Natalie. They invented trickery."

"And students surpass their teachers every day," Mathieu added, and Xavier made a sound in the back of his throat as he turned to walk away. "Right you are that the Council can't be trusted or easily tricked, but we can't just sit on our hands. Running will solve even less than trying our luck at playing the Council's game and winning. They aren't Gods. They are wolves, just like you and me, Xavier."

Xavier said nothing in response, but I could understand his anxiety. He didn't know what was coming. What he also didn't know was that what was coming was much worse than he could imagine. I sighed and closed my eyes, wishing I could remove the burden on my shoulders. but Adolfa had trusted me to carry it.

"We don't have any more time to debate this," I mumbled as I opened my eyes. "They're here." Xavier spun around, and he tilted his head to listen to the car that was pulling into the driveway outside. "Whatever happens," I whispered, "neither you nor Axel can reject Ruby. She's weak in that sense. She'll die."

"I have no plans to reject her, Natalie," Xavier said, and I nodded and turned away.

We made our way outside in time to see the door of the SUV that had arrived open. A woman stepped out, and I instantly knew she was an Enchanted like me. It was more than just the fact that her hair was white like mine, plaited in a single braid down her back. I could sense her power.

She stepped back somewhat as a foot appeared out of the car, and then a man stepped out. While I refrained from expressing the frown I felt tugging at the corner of my lips, Xavier could not. Instead of the Council representative we all expected to see, before us stood one of the three actual Council members - Olcan Crescent, the Council member for North and South America. He had come in person, which even I hadn't foreseen, and it meant this would be harder than I thought. I should have known this would be a matter he'd want to handle himself.

Mathieu stepped forward to shake Olcan's hand. "Olcan, my brother, I hadn't expected your visit."

Olcan's eyes were deep blue at the outer rim, leading into a paler blue and then brown just around his pupils. He wasn't as bulky as Mathieu, but he was just as tall, with his head shaved clean. The Enchanted stood close behind him, but her chocolate eyes were on me. With her white hair and dark skin that was glowing from the early morning sun, she exuded an ethereal beauty.

"Is that so?" Olcan said as his eyes drifted to me, and he released Mathieu's hand.

"I find it hard to believe you weren't told about us coming," the Enchanted said, her eyes on me, and I refrained from arching a brow or narrowing my eyes. I could not tell if I was hearing hostility in her deep voice or not.

"This must be Natalie," Olcan said as he approached me to shake my hand, his eyes narrowed as he looked me up and down.

"It's a pleasure to meet you, Mr. Crescent."

I held his stare. He nodded, as if with approval, and released my hand. Why should I look away or act cowardly? Mathieu had been right. The Council is made up of wolves, not Gods. If only they knew what real Gods looked like...

He then turned to Xavier, who was standing beside me and took his hand. "And you must be Xavier."

Xavier shook his hand firmly. "Welcome to our pack, Mr. Crescent. I hope your flight was a smooth one."

"It was." The side of Olcan's mouth curved as he spoke. "It was. And if it wasn't, this was still a...*necessary* trip."

Olcan turned away to stand by the Enchanted's side, and Xavier narrowed his eyes at him, then her. He glanced over at me before looking her way once more. "You're an Enchanted, yes?"

She nodded. "I am—you can see that from my hair. However, not many Enchanteds have white hair, especially young ones." Her eyes drifted to me as she said that, and this time, I arched a brow in response.

From what I understood, the stronger the Enchanted, the more white in their hair. She could sense the strength of my power when I should be nothing but a fledgling, so that comment was a jab at me. She looked to be in her early thirties, so she was young to have white hair as well.

"Well!" Olcan said as he clapped his hands, calling attention to himself. "I'm famished. Mathieu, how about we have a meal and catch up until the human arrives?"

Xavier stepped forward, a growl leaving his lips as he pinned Olcan with a glare. I quickly grabbed his arm and squeezed. Xavier wasn't one for talking, much like his father. Xavier, however, did not have his father's self-control. The corner of Olcan's mouth curved even further as he stared at Xavier, unbothered by his disrespect. It was never smart to growl at a Council member.

However, it was all part of Olcan's plan. He could easily see just how on edge Xavier seemed and would try to play on that. He would provoke Xavier to say or do anything that might show just how emotional he is because of a mere human. I had warned him about this.

"Pardon my son, Mr. Crescent," Mathieu quickly added. "We won't beat around the bush. We know why you are here and, as you know, this is a sensitive matter for everyone involved, including the Council."

Olcan tilted his head to the side at that. "I assure you, while this is, indeed, a sensitive matter, it's different for everyone involved." He gestured towards the door. "Shall we?"

Mathieu stepped aside and allowed him to pass before glancing over at Xavier. A silent message was passed between them, a clear warning telegraphed in Mathieu's expression. Xavier turned and left with both men.

I sighed and began to make my way inside as well. Thankfully, the introductions had gone smoothly (or as smoothly as could be expected under the circumstances). I was exhausted, although I was sure I was hiding it well. Locating Ruby and then projecting myself into her mind from such a distance had been taxing. I had only just woken up and had immediately started on my hunt to find her. I had woken up in the middle of the woods miles outside of town and had to hitch a ride with a trunk driver.

I was certain the truck driver had been worried about my mental health since I had sat there, spine straight with my eyes closed. Getting control over my newfound strength had been hard, especially at first, but I had no choice but to push myself. Time was running out.

"Wait," the Enchanted said behind me, and I paused, pulled from my thoughts. I turned to face her, and she walked forward to stand a step away from me. "There is something off about you. I can sense it. How does an Enchanted so young have so much power? More than many seasoned Enchanteds I know." She looked at my hair. "Who are you?"

"You know who I am. I'm Natalie, and that's all. You know some of us are born with more power than others."

This was indeed true, but maybe not the whole truth. I didn't know this woman, and I didn't trust her to tell her what really happened to me. Not yet.

"I can sense your power as well," I said to her. "You know something is coming, don't you?"

She didn't respond, but she didn't look away either, her dark eyes piercing into mine. "Yes." She finally said under her breath. "I can feel something coming. I just don't know what it is as of yet." She stepped closer to me, our faces only inches apart. Her skin was flawless, her plump lips covered in a light tint of red. "However, I have a feeling you do."

My mouth stretched with a small smile as I turned and walked away. I didn't hear her following me as I entered the house and went up the stairs.

She might be a fellow Enchanted, but she worked for the Council. I wasn't going to trust her until she proved that I could. I stopped walking abruptly as I looked down the stairs, my fingers drumming on the railing. Maybe I was thinking about this the wrong way. Maybe I was the one that needed to prove to her that she could trust me—that she could trust us.

No doubt she would be the one conducting the mind link between Ruby, Axel, and Xavier to prove they are mated. Her word was valued by the Council, clearly. Looking at this situation from the outside, you have the anomaly of Xavier having a human mate, and now there is also me, an Enchanted that's much too strong for her age. If I were her, I'd be intrigued with the Bloodmoon Pack, and maybe not in a good way.

I continued up the stairs and ran into Xavier, his eyes black pits as he stared back at me.

I sighed and cocked my head to the side for him to follow me. "Where are they?"

"Dad is giving him a tour of the grounds and of our training area. There hasn't been a report of an out of control supernatural posing a threat to the humans, but Dad wants to show him that we are still training and staying alert."

I looked over my shoulder and even though his voice was low and controlled, his eyes were still black. He was pissed, and I didn't need him doing something stupid.

"Isn't it funny how so long ago all wolf packs worked to protect humans? We were their protectors from other supernaturals that wanted them for food or whatever else. Now only a handful of packs protect them." I opened the door to Mathieu's soundproof office and locked the door behind me after Xavier entered. "Now wolves hunt them, too."

Xavier immediately started pacing. I approached him slowly and held my hand out.

"I can help."

He glanced at me and looked away. "No. I can handle it. That fucker is on our land and is about to stir shit up. Yet Dad is acting like he's just a relative visiting or something."

"Xavier, they have known each other since childhood."

"I don't care!" He yelled back at me, and I sighed and walked away to sit down. "He's here to cause trouble, to send us all to jail or worse, to kill us and Ruby. This isn't a peaceful visit. I hate acting."

I shrugged as I crossed my legs. "You're bad at it, too."

He stopped pacing to give me a nasty look and shook his head. His eyes returned to their normal color as he finally sat down and ran his hands down his face as he exhaled heavily. We sat in silence, and my eyes soon closed as my body and mind started to fall asleep.

"Enchanteds can see into the future sometimes, right?" Xavier asked, and I cracked an eye open.

"Yes. Why?"

He leaned forward, and I dreaded the question he was going to ask next. My parents had passed when I was young, and so Xavier and I had grown up like brother and sister. He could always tell when I lie.

"Do you know what's going to happen with Ruby? You're different. Natalie. Stronger, I can see it. Can you see into the future? Because I have a feeling you can."

I closed my eye again and laid down on the sofa. "Enchanteds can, and I've tried. I can't see her future. Maybe it has something to do with the block in her mind."

"Maybe you can get through it now that you're stronger. Not being able to see her future.... maybe means she...does not have one?"

I nodded, and my voice was low with sleep as I said. "I don't think so Xavier, and I wouldn't suggest you think like that. This is new territory for us all. We don't know what's right from wrong with her and this mate-bond you three have. Let's focus on keeping her out of the Council's paws."

He grunted, and I listened as the chair he was sitting on made a creaking sound from his weight. "She's coming here, from what Olcan said. I think they already have her in their paws."

I fell silent. Even after five minutes turned to fifteen and Xavier left the room, I still was wide awake. My eyes opened and I clenched my fists, as a tear fell from my eye and onto the sofa. Of course, I had seen Ruby's future. I had seen everyone's future. Even though it was all only one *possible* future, it was still enough to have me curling into a ball and crying until sleep finally took me.

CHAPTER FIVE
RUBY

Axel woke me up while it was still dark outside and ordered me to take a bath. He gave me new clothes, told me to brush my hair, and then gave me toasted bread and an apple before dragging me outside.

The cold air nipped at my exposed arms and face as we walked briskly to a black SUV. My eyes danced from left to right but it was useless to try to see anything. It was too dark for me to make out anything other than the house we had just left.

He opened the door for me, which had been surprising. I had expected him to throw me into the backseat blindfolded and handcuffed with the way he's been treating me, yanking and throwing me around as if I'm a bag of potatoes. After two and a half hours after driving what seemed like endlessly, I realized where he was taking me.

The sun had finally come up, and the world around me was finally visible. We were heading back to the Blackmoon Pack. I could tell that's where we were going the second we drove past the Witches Brew Tavern Xavier had taken me to what seemed like so long ago. More and more things began to look familiar to me, and I felt like decades had passed since I'd seen this place.

I sighed and unclenched my hands. I glanced over at Axel, who had one hand on the steering wheel and the other on the door, a deep crease between his brows. Moving my mouth from side to side and I wondered if I should speak to him, but I didn't want him to pull over and throw me into the trunk.

Fuck it.

"Why are you doing this?" I asked, and I stared at his jaw as it visibly clenched.

"Have you forgotten what I said? I told you–no talking."

I made a face, my mouth turning downward. "You told me not to speak to anyone. I didn't realize that meant you as well."

"It did," he responded sharply, and I looked back at the road.

I started to hum when I got to the point where I felt like I would lose my mind if I had to suffer one more moment of awkward silence. In my peripheral vision, I saw him glance over at me. If looks could kill, I'd be a dead woman by now, so I folded my lips inwards and fell silent once more.

I was smiling on the inside, however. He deserved to be annoyed, the smug prick. I spent the first part of the ride in a panic, thinking he was taking me to the Council. Now that I knew he was taking me back to Xavier, I felt a burst of energy, of hope.

I turned to look out the window as a thought occurred to me. Natalie had said the Council was going after Xavier. Had they arrived yet? Had she gotten to him in time? Was that why Axel was taking me back? Was the Council at Xavier's house and waiting for us?

I swallowed and closed my eyes. Of course, he hadn't had a change of heart. He wasn't returning me. He was turning me in. I opened my eyes and glanced over at him again, a loose strand of curly hair brushing against the side of his face.

"Why are you doing this, Axel? Why do you hate me so much?" His grip on the steering wheel tightened, but I didn't look away. I kept staring at him to show him I wanted an answer. "Well?"

"Humans are all the same. They are all selfish and greedy, and they can't be trusted. You *have* done something to me, Ruby. You exist." His words hit a nerve, and I narrowed my eyes at him. "You're my mate, and that's a problem. That's THE problem."

I looked away as I shook my head. I couldn't believe this man was so ignorant and biased. "You see, the thing about what you just said is," I turned to him as he glanced my way, "if I had met you before Xavier, I would have said all werewolves were cruel, cold monsters. But you and Xavier are the perfect examples to show that not all werewolves are the same. You don't get to speak generally about humans being bad. The same way I can't about werewolves." I looked away. "All the things you just listed about humans are qualities you've shown me so far. You're selfish, greedy, and you can't be trusted."

I placed my elbow on the edge of the door by the window and sighed as my skin pressed onto the cool glass. The car was filled with silence once more, and this time I intended to stay quiet. I hadn't asked to be this man's mate, and I didn't want to be his mate. He abducted me, kept me locked away in a dungeon, starved me, and dragged me through the woods. All because I have wronged him by simply *existing*.

I didn't want to believe that everything he just said was what he truly believed. He could not possibly be that ignorant. Maybe he was trying to convince himself of all that?

"My pack is my priority," he suddenly said. "Protecting them is the singular purpose I have. Therefore, I can't strengthen my bloodline by being with you, a human." He spat the last word out like it was akin to being an incurable disease.

Since I'm sure strengthening a bloodline means having kids, I can assure you of one thing, buddy, I will have zero impact. There's no way I'm opening these legs for you.

That's what I wanted to say, but I kept quiet instead. For the first time, he was speaking to me as if he was talking to another person. He wasn't giving me orders or talking down to me, and I couldn't help looking at him.

His expression was still one that screamed 'talk to me and get punched,' but his voice didn't hold as much exasperation. However, I didn't respond. I couldn't fault him for looking out for his pack's interests, but I was certain there were other ways for us to handle this situation without resorting to abduction and involving the Council.

"Who was the man that came into my cell?" I asked after a while.

He looked over at me, a confused look on his face as he shook his head. "What man? I was the only one that visited you in your cell."

Had I been hallucinating or dreaming? No, someone else had visited me.

"There was someone else. I know that was real."

The car slowed at a stoplight, and his hand fell away from the steering wheel. "I remember you asking who else would be coming to see you and I found it odd. No one else was allowed inside the cell, Ruby. Whoever was there wasn't from my pack."

The light changed to green, and he drove off as the side of my mouth curved with a smile. "Maybe now you'll understand how it feels to have people sneak onto your land."

"The land the Blackmoon Pack is on *is* my land!"

I rolled my eyes. That was none of my business. I had bigger things to think about, like if I'm about to be killed thanks to him. The closer we got to the pack, the worse my anxiety grew. Not knowing what was about to happen with my own life wasn't a comfortable feeling. I had no idea what was going to happen in the next hour, and I knew if I asked Axel, he wouldn't tell me.

"What did the man look like?" He suddenly asked, and I frowned.

That's what he's still thinking about?

"I don't know, Axel. He remained in the shadows. I didn't see his face."

He didn't say anything else, and we drove in silence for the rest of the journey. I tried to hide my excitement as Axel drove up the long path to the house. My mind took me back to the first time I had gone out with Xavier, and a bittersweet feeling had my eyes stinging with tears. In the beginning, I had wanted to get away from this place, from Xavier, and now this was the only placeI wanted to be.

Axel parked the car in front of the house. I hurriedly got out and began making my way to the door. He remained at my heel, however, not allowing me to get too far away from him. The front door was thrown open the moment I reached out to grab the handle, and Natalie grabbed my arm and pulled me into a huge hug.

She cupped my cheeks and bent my head from side to side as if inspecting me, and I allowed her to. I was too stunned at how different she looked to do anything else anyways. Her eyes drifted to Axel standing close behind me, and I smiled as she narrowed her eyes at him.

I was sure Axel wasn't bothered by the hatred dripping off her, but I was happy to finally be with someone other than him and his nasty mood. Her hands fell away from my cheeks as she took my hand and began leading us inside and into the living room.

My heart felt heavy as my eyes wandered around a house that I hadn't been sure I'd ever see again. I was happy and scared all at once, and the mixture of feelings had me feeling sick. Those feelings vanished though, when we entered the living room, and my eyes found Xavier.

He was standing by Mathieu's side and, while I knew there were two other people present that I didn't know, I couldn't tear my eyes away from Xavier. It felt like I hadn't seen him in years, and my fingers began to twitch with my need to feel his warm skin.

My heart was beating so fast, it felt like it would beat its way out of my chest. I didn't care that everyone in the room could hear it.

You're okay.

"Xavier..." I whispered as I stepped forward, but Axel grabbed my elbow almost painfully and yanked me back to him.

"What did I tell you?" He whispered in my ear. "Speak to no one."

Xavier's growl rolled through the room like a clap of thunder. He moved forward and was halfway across the room in a flash, his eyes obsidian. Axel shoved me behind him as he widened his stance for Xavier's attack, his nails changing into claws.

The man I didn't know appeared between the two of them in the blink of an eye. Xavier stopped, his chest rising and falling rapidly, his eyes still on Axel.

"Now, now, now," the man said as he looked from Axel to Xavier, "there won't be any fighting. It is interesting, however, how two alphas-to-be are willing to rip each other apart for this," he looked at me with obvious disdain, "girl."

I made a face, not liking the way he had just said that, and he walked over to me. He looked me up and down, his nostrils flaring. I watched in confusion as he glanced over at the woman I didn't know.

She, too, was looking at me, her dark eyes piercing into my green ones.

Who are these people? Are they from the Council?

I narrowed my eyes at the man as he stepped back, the light from the bulb above us causing his bald head to glisten. *Of course, they are from the Council. They must be.*

I looked at Mathieu who was silently staring daggers at Xavier. "Xavier," he called and Xavier stood up straight, his eyes returning to their normal color.

"Axel has her in his possession, so he has the right to do what he wishes. She is his mate as well, is she not?"

"That's bullshit and you know it!" Xavier yelled.

"Xavier!" Mathieu said again, this time louder, as he got to his feet. "That's enough."

Xavier's jaws clenched as he bowed his head. "With all due respect, Father, Axel can't be making rules off the top of his head if this is something that has never happened before."

Mathieu approached his son and placed his hand on his shoulder. "This is new territory, so it's best to let the Council do what they think is necessary. She *is* his mate as well, Xavier." Xavier made a sound, and Mathieu squeezed his shoulder. I felt so useless, a lamb amongst wolves, and feared what would happen if I opened my mouth again. "He is. We all want this over and done with."

The bald man waved his hand, beckoning to the woman with white hair. She went to him obediently. *Are they mates, I wonder?*

"Indeed, we all want this over with. I've seen enough for today, Mathieu. My flight was long, and tomorrow is going to be an even longer day—for all of us. Thank you for giving me a tour of the grounds, but I think I'm going to get some rest before dinner."

He turned and left the room, and I didn't miss the way he glanced at me from the side. I didn't like this man. Each time he looked at me, I got a terrible feeling like snakes were crawling all over me. I looked toward Natalie, who had remained by my side throughout the whole ordeal, but she merely held my hand and squeezed it before turning away.

I moved to reach out to her, and Axel cleared his throat, causing my hand to freeze mid-air. I looked at him and forced as much distaste into my eyes and expression as possible. I was out of that cell and room he had kept me in, but somehow, he still had chains on me. My eyes found Xavier once more, and a feeling of warmth came over me as I looked into his eyes, the longing I could see there.

I hadn't realized just how much I had missed him until this very moment.

"Let's go," Axel said through clenched teeth, but I remained still. "Now."

Xavier's eyes shot down to my arm as Axel held onto me, and it felt like a knife was twisting in my chest as he then looked away. His demeanor changed instantly, and I could almost see a wall appear between us. I yanked my hand away from Axel, but Xavier was already walking out of the room.

A deafening silence filled the room as my heart fell and shattered. I looked behind me at Mathieu, a plea in my eyes, but he only shook his head.

"I'm sorry, child, but this will all be over soon."

CHAPTER SIX
XAVIER

As the night stretched on, I felt more and more awake. I rolled onto my back and stared up at the ceiling, but I was so lost in thought that I wasn't really seeing it.

Somewhere in the house was Ruby, so close, yet still so far out of my reach. *Is she asleep? Is she awake? Is she sleeping in the same bed as Axel?*

That last thought had me clenching and unclenching my fists as I rolled onto my stomach, causing my sheet to roll down to my waist. The cool night air blew into the room through the open window, and I inhaled deeply as it chilled my exposed back. When I had seen Ruby today, a part of my world that had been in ruins for a week instantly mended itself. That is until that asshole Axel had put his hands on her.

The rage I had felt on the night I had saved Ruby in that alleyway so many weeks ago returned in a crashing wave. I had wanted to rip Axel to shreds. My skin dotted with goosebumps the moment she entered the house and I could smell her. But when I saw her, I felt like killing someone.

Her skin was still smooth and unmarred and her hair still a vivid red, but she was thinner. Her collar bones and shoulder blades were so pronounced. She had lost so much I could barely believe she had only been gone a week.

I rolled out of bed, my temper getting the better of me the more I thought about what she might have gone through. I threw a shirt on and made my way downstairs and into the kitchen to grab a bottle of water. Sitting through dinner with my dad, Olcan, and his Enchanted, Rieka, had been painful. I had hoped Axel would join us along with Ruby, but they had remained in their room.

I still think it is rubbish that Olcan was allowing Axel to keep Ruby away from me. Yes, he's her mate, but so am I. I hated the way he had said "She's in Axel's possession," as if he was talking about a mere object and not a person. What's worse was that I had no idea what plans he had for Ruby, myself, and my dad. What I fear most is being forced to reject her.

Maybe that's what Natalie had meant when she had said the Council would try to see what effect she has on Axel and me. Right now, I was more worried about Ruby than myself.

Natalie didn't have to tell me Ruby wouldn't be able to take it. Then again, she might not feel anything, while I felt it all. When our bond was discovered, she got sick, but the almost paralyzing need that came after wasn't something she seemed to feel. Maybe if Axel or I rejected her, she'd merely feel sick again and then get over it.

I threw the empty water bottle in the recycle bin and began making my way through the house to go outside. It was a tranquil night with a clear sky and a calming breeze. I sorely needed something calming right now.

My plan to relax outside until I felt sleepy crumbled to the ground as I stepped out the door and saw Axel standing outside. I paused, my eyes lowering with annoyance, but I wasn't about to turn and go back inside. This was my house.

I pulled up by his side, but neither of us spoke. He dropped the cigarette he was smoking and crushed it under his boot before blowing out a cloud of smoke.

"Why did you do this?" I asked him. "Why did you tell the Council about Ruby? She's your mate as well, Axel. Do you really not have a soul to feel anything when you think about her getting hurt?"

He didn't respond, and we both kept staring dead ahead. An owl hooted in the distance as the trees swayed in the winds, and I finally looked over at him. He was older than me, but clearly not wiser if he thought this bullshit move was a good idea.

"All we needed was time to get some answers because you and I both know the Council won't show her mercy." He looked at me from the corner of his eyes. "You've fucked us all over, and for what?"

"How long would it have taken for us to get any answers? Huh?" He asked. "The Council will do that, and faster."

"The Council will search for a reason to kill her! She's a human that's mated to us both!"

He turned to face me, a deep crease between his brows as he pointed a finger at my face. We're about the same height, and while he might be older with more fighting experience, he wasn't as pissed off as I was.

"She's your mate, Blackwood, not mine. I'm sick of saying that. Do you want to know why I'm doing this?" He stepped closer to me, and my nose twitched at the smell of the cigarette on his breath. "You're weak, and she's making you weaker. You'll have to take over for your dad soon, and you are nowhere near ready. You're not built to be an alpha."

"You don't know shit about me," I said through clenched teeth, and he chuckled mockingly.

"I know more than you think. Alphas are supposed to put their pack before everything and everyone. A single human knowing about us can be detrimental, and just because she's your mate, you spared her. What, Xavier, are you going to make her Luna for the pack? Is she going to bear your pups? Can she even survive a werewolf pregnancy? You haven't thought about any of this, that much is clear. Doing this saves her, Xavier, or she's going to live a life of rejection and pain. When it comes right down to it, you can't make the tough decisions. Rejecting a mate is the hardest thing for any wolf to do, but an alpha must be prepared to do it. She won't just be your woman, she'll be your pack's Luna. It will be her job to birth the next alpha. Have you ever heard of a half human and half wolf child becoming an alpha?"

I said nothing, and he made a sound and turned away while shaking his head. I swallowed hard. Everything he had said was true, and of course, I've thought about those things. But like I'd said, we just needed time to know what we're dealing with. Maybe he's right, I'm not ready to be an alpha. One thing is for sure, I am not ready now, nor will I ever be ready to be the man that kills his mate.

"It'll kill her. You know rejecting her might kill her, don't you? But hey, you don't care. Tell me, Axel, what choice does she have in all of this? If you don't want her, fine, that's great news. But just leave us alone then. Don't preach to me about what I should want, or what's good for my pack. My people are different from yours, and always have been."

He crossed his hands over his chest. "Goddess, do you even hear yourself?" He shook his head and looked down at the crushed cigarettes on the ground. "You know what, you're not my problem. Olcan will handle it. Ruby is just a means to an end for my pack to return to these lands."

My head tilted to the side. This man was talking about me not being a true alpha when he was putting my pack, his pack, and an innocent girl's life at risk, all for some land?

"That's what this is about? Land? Are you serious, Axel? You can take your pack anywhere, *anywhere,* and you've brought the Council here because of greed?"

He spun around to face me, his eyes blazing with anger.

"Greed? This is my land! My pack's land! We deserve to live here! You have no idea how hard it is to relocate or even find suitable land to hide werewolves. My people have made their lives here. They live comfortably enough among the humans, but we have to live somewhere with trees, thick trees so we can be comfortable. So we don't have to fear shifting and being caught."

This time I stepped forward, my face inches away from his. I wasn't going to be challenged or disrespected on my land. His pack left ours years ago, the decisions made by people in the past were none of my business. Not right now.

"For years our packs have come to an agreement and have lived peacefully *away* from each other. Now you want to start a war over this, and you've included the Council that you think is only going to stick to one matter and not dig deeper into our lives. So that's it, you wanna use Ruby to give the Council a reason to say we are a weak pack, that we don't deserve this land? What about your pack, Axel? Do you think the Council doesn't know about your wild pack members that had attacked those humans?" I shook my head. This man was delusional. "You've fucked yourself, Axel, and your people, too. The Council might hate humans like you do, but they don't tolerate dumb shit like that."

His face twisted, and I realized I had hit a nerve. Of course, he didn't know that bit of information had gotten out. My lips curved into a sinister smile.

"The wolves that did that were taken care of." He said slowly.

"Do you think the Council will care? They'll just say you don't have a strong enough hold on your people for that to have *ever* happened to begin with. All you do is spew hatred for humans, so of course, your pack members will act wrongfully because of the bullshit you fed them. Where the fuck is your father? If I'm not ready to be alpha, then neither are you. Where is your father? You're not alpha yet, and a true alpha doesn't resort to trickery or go as far as to abduct another's mate."

"She's not only your mate, but she's also mine as well, remember?"

My gums began to ache as my need to rip his throat out grew stronger. This man didn't even know what he wanted. One minute he claimed she wasn't his mate and then the next minute he claimed she was. Ruby didn't deserve that, and he did not deserve her.

"She is, but she'll never choose you! She'll never choose you!" I looked him up and down, my face twisted with disgust. "You'll always be a savage, no matter what land you and your pack live on." I flicked my finger under my nose as his cigarette breath became unbearable. For werewolves, every sense is heightened. I have no idea how or why he smokes those things. "Where is Alpha Sirhan? He knows this isn't how wolves act. This isn't the way we handle things. Humans behave like this. They go behind each other's backs, so their wars never end. But wolves are *better*. We work things out civilly to keep the peace."

I stepped back and made a sound, one to show my repulsion, while he continued to stare at me, his lips in a thin line. I knew that, even in the current situation, his father, Alpha Sirhan, would never condone an action such as abducting someone's mate. It was an unthinkable act of hostility and aggression.

"You act like you know everything. You stand there and judge me as if you're better than me. What kind of alpha has Sirhan raised? You're acting more human than wolf. You're a fucking disappointment!"

I saw his fist coming, but he had moved so quickly I hadn't had the time to dodge it. His fist connected with my jaw, sending me staggering backward, but I caught my balance quickly. My hand shifted and swiped at his chest, cutting through his shirt and chest.

He howled in pain and dove for me, his shirt ripping off his body as he began to shift when Olcan appeared before him. Olcan slapped Axel across the face, sending him flying backward.

I stared in shock at Olcan's strength, while Axel skidded to a stop on the ground. He had backhanded Axel as easily as if he were swatting a fly.

He turned to face me; his eyes black. "You two are both disappointments." His voice was low, his expression neutral, but his words were dripping with rage. "I had hoped we could all stay under the same roof for one night. I wanted to see what hold that girl has on you both, on two promising alphas. Look at you!" He looked over his shoulder at Axel, who had finally gotten onto his feet, his chest already healing. "You were both ready to fight each other, to kill each other, for a human. You both failed my test miserably. Whom would she fight for either of you?"

"Olcan, I..."

"Silence!" He yelled at me as my father appeared outside as well. He pointed a stern finger at me. "I've had enough of your attitude. Do not speak unless spoken to, wolf! Know your place!"

I turned to look at my dad, and the weariness in his eyes had me swallowing what response I was about to give Olcan. I don't care about Olcan or Axel, but disappointing my father was the last thing I wanted to do. I'm his one and only son. His only heir to carry on the Blackwood name. I was making a fool of myself and of our pack.

Natalie had warned us that this would happen, that the Council would watch us closely to see what effect Ruby has on us. This wasn't Ruby's fault. This was Axel's fault and my own. Frankly, it was more his fault than mine. *He* was the one who invited the Council.

"Do you want to know what I've seen so far?" Olcan said to no one in particular as he walked away, his hand on his chin. "I see two men who aren't ready to be alphas."

"Olcan, this isn't..." Axel began to say but clamped his mouth shut as Olcan growled at him.

Olcan pointed a finger at Axel and then at me. "Neither of you is ready. You're both too emotional. Despite what issues are between your fathers, have they ever behaved like this? Sure, this is a little different, because you both have the same mate. But do you really?" I frowned at him, and he shrugged. "Is she really mated to you both? I would have liked a good night's sleep, but I guess that won't be happening." He turned to my father. "Wake her up. We're having the trial tonight."

⊷• ❦ •⊶

NATALIE

I watched Xavier make his way outside and knew disaster was about to strike. I remained by the window on the second floor, his and Axel's conversation floating up to me on the cool wind.

I listened as their conversation grew more heated and knew this was what Olcan wanted. Xavier had been ready to rip Axel to shreds today when he had arrived with Ruby, and Olcan had left Ruby under Axel's care for the sole purpose of seeing how Xavier would react. Would he remain cool and collected, or act on his instincts to be with his mate and not have another man touching her.

Of course, Axel wasn't just another man, and that would bother Xavier even more.

It was a setup. I knew I was right to think so as soon as Axel punched Xavier and Olcan made his appearance to lecture them both. I had expected Xavier to throw the first punch, but I had been wrong. However, I was just as curious as Xavier was about Axel's father. Axel was here alone when his father's presence as alpha was needed as well.

That was strange, but really none of my concern.

"She's a lucky girl," I heard Reika say behind me.

"How so?" I asked, and she appeared by the window to stare down at the men.

"She has two alphas fighting over her. A Council member making an appearance in person that we all know is dangerous for him and a powerful Enchanted as a friend." She looked over at me. "I'd say she's a lucky girl."

I turned to stare at her, and she gave me a teasing smile. "I'd say she's a girl that didn't pick any of this and wants it to end like everyone else."

"Well," she looked away, "I'll see for myself if that's true. Apparently sooner rather than later."

I looked back down at the men, and my ears perked up as Olcan announced that he'd be conducting the trial tonight. I sighed and swallowed hard.

"What will you do to her?"

Reika moved her hair behind her ears as she turned her back to the window. "A mind link. From what I've been told, you tried and learned nothing. For an Enchanted so strong, how was that possible?"

I wasn't about to answer that. "And if it doesn't work for you either, what then?"

She shrugged. "Olcan will decide. Take comfort in knowing that he actually likes Ruby."

I turned my back to the window as well. "Does he? Why? I'd think he'd despise her. She's creating chaos- although indirectly of course."

"Of course." She drawled before looking over at me. "Olcan has yet to find his mate and is quite the man whore. He thinks she's beautiful, *but* he's also very intrigued by this entire thing." She turned to face me, a new fire within her eyes. "Imagine what will happen if this gets out? A human mated to a wolf." She smiled. "There is no known record of hybrids. We have no idea what a child between a human and a wolf would be like. Axel thinks it will weaken a wolf's bloodline."

"Don't you think so?"

She inhaled deeply and turned around to look up at the night sky. "What I think doesn't matter." She murmured before looking down at me. "What I think, Natalie, is that if this isn't some kind of witch's trick, what Olcan has planned is going to really piss our goddess off."

"And what does he have planned?" I asked her, my eyes piercing into her, but she began walking away.

"Let's just say there might be a spike in hybrid children if they prove to be strong. That's if the human mothers can even handle the pregnancy. That, I will never stand for."

CHAPTER SEVEN
RUBY

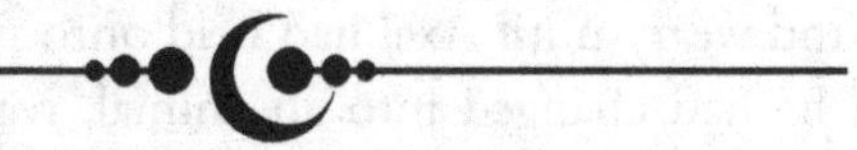

I had pretended to be sleeping when Axel called me. He could probably tell I wasn't sleeping, and so he only called me twice before giving up and leaving the room. I plopped over onto my back the moment the door closed and sighed with relief. I was finally alone.

Immediately after eating dinner (proper food might I add, and not just scraps like Axel had been feeding me), I had climbed into bed. Axel had given me the bed to myself while he slept on the couch in the room. *Maybe there's a working heart inside his chest after all.*

I had expected him to tell me to sleep on the floor.

No matter how comfortable the bed was, the hours ticked by, and I still couldn't drift off to sleep. I was too anxious and too scared of what was going to happen when the sun rose again.

Olcan, that's the name of the bald man I had met when I had arrived. He definitely gave me the creeps, and not just because of his strange eyes. It was the way he looked at me. I felt like he had been trying to see inside me, and I didn't like it. The Enchanted with him, however, she might actually be able to see inside my mind, the way Natalie had tried. Would she be able to break through whatever wall was there? Natalie hadn't been able to, and I'd be lying if I said I wasn't curious to know what was there. What had I placed under such a secure lock and key that not even I could remember?

Xavier's face flashed in my mind, and I called out to the image as it slipped away. His face reappeared, and I sank further into the bed. A heavy sadness rested in my heart. It had felt like the air had been sucked out of my chest when I had seen him. He had looked tired and weary until Axel had held onto me and pulled me back. Then he had changed into an animal, ready to rip anyone who stood between us to shreds.

He would do that for me, and a smile curved the corner of my lips. I wished I could get out of bed and go find him right now, but with Olcan and his Enchanted around, I didn't want to do anything to give them more reason to dislike me.

I got out of bed to get a glass of water from the bathroom, my feet pattering on the cold tile. I stared at myself in the mirror, dark circles under my eyes, and my sadness grew worse. Why had Xavier looked away like that earlier? He looked as if he had just given up and left me to Axel. I felt like a piece of meat being thrown around for everyone to take a bite.

In a few hours, Olcan would be taking his bite. I splashed water onto my face to try and wash away the horrible images being created in my mind. No, Xavier won't let that man kill me. I have to believe that.

I made my way back into the room to lay across the bed towards the open window. Resting my chin in the palm of my hand, I tried to remember the voice of the man that had visited me before Axel. If he wasn't one of Axel's men, who was he?

His dislike for me had been clear, but I suppose I can only add him to the growing list of people that want me gone. According to him, wolves never thought they could be mated to humans. Now I felt like agreeing. Look at the stress that has been dished out to me for something that neither I nor the wolves have any control over.

Yet still, I'm being treated as if this is all on me. You'd think I had stolen something from them, spilled their secrets, or had committed murder.

I was sick of the back and forth. One minute I felt like this life might not be so bad, and then right as I became comfortable enough to give this all a chance, the rug was pulled right out from under me yet again.

I pressed my face into the sheet and screamed as loud as I could. I didn't care if anyone could hear. I liked Xavier so much, but being with him, or the thought of being with him, was only causing heartache. I knew without a doubt if anything was to happen to him, Natalie, Mathieu, or the pack in general because of me, I'd never recover. If I had to choose between Xavier's pack and Axel's, Xavier deserved to be left alone, and he should be applauded for saving a life, especially since that life belonged to his mate. That's not how this world works, however.

No good deed goes unpunished. That saying isn't just for humans. It works that way for werewolves as well.

I sighed and turned onto my side; my knees pulled up to my chest. Whatever happens, happens. I just hope no one dies, including myself.

Two knocks came at the door, and my heart skipped two beats simultaneously with the knocks. I fisted my blouse at my chest as a sick feeling began to spread through my body. I climbed off the bed and made my way to the door, praying that beyond it stood Xavier. I flipped the switch to turn the lights on before ruffling my hair and pinching my cheeks for some color I knew I was lacking. However, when I swung the door open, my shoulders immediately dropped with disappointment.

"Well, you don't have to look that disappointed," Natalie said as she entered the room, her white hair blowing behind her like a curtain.

I closed the door and returned to bed. "I'm not."

"Oh, you and I both know who you wanted it to be standing

outside the door. Don't front, Ruby." She sat on the edge of the bed. "I didn't think you'd be awake."

"I can't sleep. Not when I know tomorrow Olcan might order someone to kill me."

"That won't happen."

I plopped down onto the bed and covered my face with my hands. "Still, I don't think anything good is going to come from that trial tomorrow. Well, today, when the sun is up. What time is it anyway?"

Natalie didn't respond and I peeked at her through my fingers. "It's two in the morning," she finally replied. She then got up off the bed, and I propped myself up on my elbows. "What did Axel do to you?"

I made a face. "I was in a dungeon for days before he dragged me to the basement of his house, where he finally had the decency to feed me scraps of food and give me some water. Something weird happened while I was in the dungeon, though. I was alone most of the time, except for a man that visited at one point. I couldn't see his face and didn't recognize his voice, but he knew about me and my mate-bond to Axel and Xavier.When I questioned Axel about it, he said no one else was allowed to see me at that time. I'm not sure what to make of that.. "

Her eyes narrowed, and she looked away. "No one else knows about this. Well, no one else *should*, unless someone's lips got a little loose."

"Do you think it's the Council?"

She shook her head and walked away, her fingers combing her hair backward. "No. Since Olcan came himself, this is serious to him. He doesn't want this getting out just yet."

"Yeah, so no one will know when I'm killed. A girl that no one knows can't be missed." Nathalie walked back over to the bed and sat down. She sighed heavily as she stared at me, and I frowned. Why did she suddenly look so gloomy? "What's wrong?"

"Axel and Xavier got into it just now. They had to be parted by Olcan.

That can't be good.

"Why were they fighting?"

She pinned me with a stare. "Do you really have to ask that?"

I smiled a little because I knew I didn't. I, however, found it hard to believe that Axel was fighting over me. Surely he was pissed about something else.

"Xavier might get angry over me, but Axel is upset about other things. I don't see how he and I are mated. I know I feel the bond differently from you guys, but it's like he feels nothing."

"Or he tries not to," she added, and I shook my head.

"Well, he has a future in acting. I can't imagine Xavier ever leaving me in a dungeon. With the way you have all said this mate thing works, I was surprised Axel could do something like that to me. Shouldn't I be feeling more?"

The side of her mouth arched upwards as she hunched her shoulders, "No one knows what you should or shouldn't be feeling. What do you feel when you're around them?"

I bit down on my lip, and a shy smile made its way onto my lips as I thought of Xavier. "I don't feel this instant overload of love, or whatever, but I feel warm and comfortable around Xavier. I know he'll do anything to protect me, he'll do anything to keep me safe." My smile fell away, and I covered my face. "Despite what Axel has done, and I do want to cut his dick off, I...I feel...protected around him. That's so fucked up considering what he's done, so maybe that's not the right word, but there is this thing about him... He's like a mean bodyguard, you know. We might argue and get on each other's nerves, but if it ever comes down to it, I know he'd protect me. That's what I feel. But then he yanks me around by my hair or leaves me without water for days, and I think he's just soulless. There's no way he can be feeling the bond."

"They both feel it, trust me. Think of it as Xavier just being more open-minded than Axel. Axel is older than Xavier, and he might have had terrible experiences with humans in the past. He's grown up in a pack that is still trying to stick to how things were immediately after the war between wolves and humans. Look at it this way - he's the alpha to be., It's a big role to fill to start with, then add in having a human Luna in a pack that hates humans, and you have a big problem. He must be stressed. If he doesn't reject you, his pack will force him to. He'll have to choose between you, or what he was born to be. That's a terrible choice for anyone to have to make."

When she explained it that way, I could understand the rock and a hard place he must be stuck between. His life had probably been going as planned for him to be the next alpha. All of a sudden, here I come, a human girl that he feels compelled to be with on a deep level, yet he can't because he has to stick to some twisted hatred passed down generation after generation.

"Yeah," I drawled. "I guess his mind must be a little effed-up right now, but that won't save him from my wrath. That bastard left me in a dungeon!"

Natalie raised her fist, and I bumped mine against it. "That's my girl. But I need you to come with me." I gave her a look, and my chest tightened as she stared back at me with regret. "He wants to do the trial tonight."

"Olcan? Why?"

I felt like the world around me froze. A chill danced down my spine as my eyes widened, and I began shaking my head. *No, no, I'm not ready. I thought I had one night to prepare myself and now this?*

"What's going to happen?" I asked. "What's the trial going to be like?"

"I wish I had time to explain, but they're waiting on us." She got up and held her hand out to me. I could only stare at it, and I knew she could hear my racing heart. "I need you to trust me. I'll be right there, Ruby, right beside you. I promise."

I had trusted Natalie from the moment I had met her. That

moment seemed so very long ago. While I was still curious to know what inspired her hair transformation, I knew hair wasn't the only thing that had changed about Nathalie in the time since I was abducted.,. From the time we first met, I had been drawn to Nathalie's spunkiness, her bubbly and chatty nature. I could consistently count on her to flash one of her charming Nathalie grins that practically touched her ears and made her eyes twinkle, and before I knew it, I'd be beaming right along with her. But now her smiles didn't even reach her eyes.

I took her hand, and she pulled me up. "Natalie, what happened?"

She blinked once, seemingly caught off guard by my question. "Nothing that didn't need to happen. I'm okay."

"Are you sure? I mean, your hair is the same as the Enchanted that came with Olcan, Reika, or whatever her name is. Coincidence?"

"Enchanteds of a certain power level have white hair."

I looked from left to right. So within the short time I had been gone, she became so much more powerful. *How?* No wonder she had been able to find me. Now wasn't the time for me to press her for answers though. Olcan was waiting, and I'd rather not piss him off before this trial even gets started. Knowing me, there would be more than enough time for that to happen later, whether I wanted to or not..

"Okay, we should go, but this conversation isn't over. I want to know what happened because I know something did."

We exited the room. I followed behind her slowly, my legs taking short steps. "I got a little help with seeing the world a bit clearer." She said almost inaudibly. "That's all. I know I'm not myself, but sometimes seeing more than you wanted or needed to see changes a person."

She stopped walking abruptly, and before I could react, she pulled me in for a hug. At first, I just stood there, shocked and mildly confused, before I wrapped my arms around her. I sank into the hug as she did, and we both sighed at the same time. While Natalie is only twenty years old to my nineteen, she has become someone that I look up to. She is an old soul, and I'm sure that was why so many people gravitated to her.

"No matter what happens tonight," she whispered. "I'm happy I met you." She pulled away but kept her hands firmly on my shoulders. "Us odd girls have to stick together."

I cupped her cheeks. "I'm ready."

<hr>

AXEL

I stood by the window with my hands buried in my pockets and my eyes glued to the starry sky. Natalie had told Mathieu she'd wake Ruby, but that was almost half an hour ago. The longer they took to come downstairs, the more irritated I grew at being forced to be in the same room as these people.

Xavier had no right to talk about my father. I'm here. I'm handling things, and that's just the way things are. How dare he act like I don't know what I'm doing? My eyes wandered from the sky to the towering trees and I clenched my jaw. This land, this entire fucking land, belongs to my people, too. We barely have enough space in the area where we've been forced to settle for years, whereas both packs could easily spread out on this land and never even come across each other in passing.

I glanced over at Xavier whispering to his father, low enough that not even I could hear. They looked at me at the same time before Xavier stood up straight and crossed his arms over his chest. I looked away, not bothered in the least by his attitude. Olcan and Reika were busy talking about a fundraiser, the two of them not bothered by Natalie and Ruby taking so long. I would have thought Olcan would have torn the house apart by now.

Was this the Council that everyone fears?

I wanted this over with. Everything had been going smoothly for me until I came to this damn house and picked up on Ruby's scent. I looked out the window before closing my eyes, my senses taking me back to that day. I had never before smelled something, someone, so mouth-watering. I had tried to picture her just by her scent, but nothing in my wildest dreams could have prepared me for those devastating green eyes, vividly red hair, and that heartbreakingly human heart.

Then I had smelt Xavier on her, and I completely lost it.

I couldn't believe my mate was human. But even more than that, I couldn't believe my mate, my other half, was also mated to another wolf. It didn't make sense to me then, and it doesn't make sense now. I never thought I'd even find my mate so soon. That has never been something I was eager about.

After meeting Ruby, however, I've felt more torn than I ever have before. I can feel her, smell her, and I constantly sense the pull of our bond. But I can't bring myself to trust her. I feel like this isn't real. A human mated to a wolf brings about so much tension, so many questions. How will a human survive a wolf pregnancy? When I do finally mate, I plan on staying that way for life. I won't become attached to someone that will just leave eventually. At this point, she's more Xavier's mate than mine anyway. She has made her choice.

That scent, that hypnotizing scent, drifted into the room, and I looked to the door as Ruby appeared with Natalie. She looked my way as she walked in. I could see the fear in her eyes, but otherwise, she appeared calm. That's something I could easily admit to admiring about her. Even in the face of danger, she puts on a brave face and tries to stand her ground.

"You ladies certainly took your time," Olcan said he took a seat and nodded to Reika. "I'm sure everyone wants this over this. So, how about we begin?"

Ruby said nothing as she held Olcan's gaze before looking at Reika, who stepped towards her. Her eyes darted to Xavier, and my hand twitched as their eyes locked. They stared at each other, an unspoken message passing between them before she looked at Reika once more.

I wasn't jealous.

Okay, I was. But at the same time, I don't want to be with her. We have zero possibility of a real future together. She is just a means to an end to get what I want. Mate or not, she's human. We'll never work out, and mate or not, Xavier broke the law to spare her.

"This will be simple and painless," Reika said as she held her hand out to Ruby. However, Ruby only looked at her hand before looking at me. I stared back at her, not sure why she was staring at me so intently. I nodded to her nonetheless. Reika shook her hand that was still outstretched, pulling Ruby's eyes away from me. "Take my hand. I'll create a mind link to see within you. That is all."

"That was already done," Xavier said. "Natalie did that, and it didn't work. There is some kind of block in her mind."

"We're here to find out who she is, Xavier, to start," Olcan replied. "That is what we will be doing."

Xavier shook his head, "Trying again might hurt her. You can't force through a block like that. It takes time, breaking it piece by piece. It should not be done by brute force."

I wasn't going to say it aloud, but I agreed with Xavier. Yes, I wanted to have this all figured out, but I didn't want Ruby to suffer unnecessarily. Wolves fear the Council so much, but they should remember that the Council is just wolves like us. They only want the best for all werewolves. The Council members over the years have remembered and held onto many of our old ways in order to secure our safety and protect our secrets. We must do so at all costs, even if it means that some lives are lost in the process.

Nevertheless, my deal with Olcan hadn't included hurting Ruby. I would reject her. Xavier would be given the choice to, though I knew rejecting her was something he'd never do. He didn't have the balls to make the tough calls for the pack. He, his father, and the entire Blackmoon pack would then be dealt with accordingly. That is what would happen here.

Though I had to admit, I was curious. How could a human girl, who was already responsible for bringing so much chaos, also be capable of sealing off her past so tightly that an Enchanted couldn't get through? What exactly had happened to her? What did she want so badly to forget?

"If something in her past was hiddenbehind such a strong block, then it must be important. Maybe it'll explain who she is, where she really came from. Maybe it'll explain why she can be mated to two wolves."

"I'm a normal girl, Axel. You keep talking about me as if I fell from the sky or something," she replied, and I shrugged.

"We'll find out soon enough, won't we?" I replied.

"Of course, you wouldn't care if she gets hurt or not," Xavier shot my way, and my brow knitted.

"I care about getting this thing over with. I don't care if..."

"Enough!" Ruby yelled, and all eyes turned to her. "Can both of you stop it?" She looked from me to Xavier. "I can handle it okay. I want to know what's locked away in my mind, hidden from even me. I can do this."

Olcan leaned forward. "Okay, that's enough. Xavier, your opinion is welcomed, but this will be done whether or not you or Ruby want it. *I* want to know who this girl is. *I* want to know if she can be trusted with our secrets. Mathieu, you've allowed a human to walk free amongst our people without knowing her true self. You should have broken through whatever wall was there before you made a decision like that. Whatever is concealed in her mind might hurt more than just your own pack. She could very well be dangerous to all wolves."

Mathieu remained reclined in his seat, his left leg crossed over the right. "She was spared because she is the mate to a wolf, human though she may be. Yes, our law is to protect our secrets at all costs.

However, I didn't think it was my place to break another even more important law in order to uphold that law. Harming another wolf's mate is punishable by death."

Xavier looked my way. I knew he was thinking - I could see it in his eyes. If only I weren't Ruby's other mate, he'd have been well within his rights to kill me with his own handsfor abducting her. If she wasn't my mate, I would have no reason to be here other than to watch the fall of the Blackmoon pack.

Olcan sat back, a cunning smirk on his lips. "Right you are, Mathieu. But," he lifted a finger, "that law is for female wolves, not humans."

No one spoke for a while as Olcan and Mathieu continued to stare at each other. Olcan was right about that, and Mathieu knew it. Olcan then looked at Reika and nodded, and she took both of Ruby's hands into hers.

"I'll help," Natalie suddenly announced as she walked up to Ruby to stand behind her. "Maybe with the two of us it won't be as much pressure on you or Ruby. We'll take this slow."

Reika stared at her for a moment before looking at Ruby, who nodded her consent. She was beginning to look more terrified, her bravado slipping, and I couldn't blame her. I'd hate to have anyone roaming around inside my head. Reika released Ruby's hands to press her fingers to Ruby's temples, while Natalie placed both hands on the sides of Ruby's head.

Natalie closed her eyes as Reika did, but Ruby's eyes remained open. I watched as she swallowed hard. I looked away, annoyed that I was starting to worry about her. This is what I hate, this connection to her that won't allow me to maintain my indifference like I want to.

Both Enchanteds began to speak under their breath, their chant growing steadily louder. Ruby's eyes fluttered close as her body grew stiff, and even Mathieu sat forward. I could not understand their words as their voices grew louder and louder, but I could feel the sudden burst of power within the room.

I stepped forward quickly but stopped myself just as Natalie and Reika stopped chanting. Then the heads of all three women fell back at the same time.

⚬•━━━━━━━━━ ┅•● ●•┅ ━━━━━━━━━•⚬

RUBY

I was on the verge of shitting myself as Reika and Natalie both held me. I had been doing my best to hide my fear, but I couldn't cover it fully any longer. These women were about to take a deep dive inside my head, and no one knew what was going to happen when they did.

I swallowed as I heard them begin to whisper words I didn't understand, and a chill went down my spine. It didn't take long for whatever they were doing to kick in because soon, my body started to feel weak and my eyes fluttered closed.

The moment my eyes closed, there was a burst of blinding light. I opened my eyes slowly as it began to die away, and I found myself standing in a white room. It was more like a box with no doors or windows, just white walls.

I looked down at my hands before touching my face and exhaling. I'll never get used to how real this all feels.

"Natalie?" I turned in a circle. "Reika?"

My echo was the only response. Within the next second, there was a loud boom, like a bomb going off, and I crunched down. The white world around me began to change. People started appearing around me, along with cars and buildings. Everything was hazy and hard to see, preventing me from making out faces or anything distinctive. All I could tell for certain was that the people running were all humans.

I was facing one way, and they were all running towards my direction, their cries and screams mingled together. They were running from something, but I couldn't tell from what. I started walking, moving out of the way to dodge them, although I knew they would just run through me in this fake reality.

What is this?

If this was a memory, when had this all happened? I stopped as a woman tripped and flipped onto her back. I couldn't tell what she was looking at, but she was crawling backward on her hands. A black shadow appeared before her, and my brows knitted. It was a shadow of another person, and as they jumped on top of her, I screamed.

As I reached out and screamed,a large crack appeared just between her and the shadow.

"Ruby!"

I spun around as Natalie called my name, and another crack appeared, followed by yet another. I looked back at the woman on the ground and the frozen shadow above her. I took a step forward, and as I did so, a sharp pain surged through my head. I hunched forward, my hand on my head, before glancing up at the shadow once more.

It was shaped like a human, but why was it black? I could tell the color of the clothes of all the humans and their complexion despite everything being hazy, so why was this human just a black shadow.

My eyes widened.

A supernatural?

"Ruby!"

This time it was Reika's voice, and then another sharp pain, worse than the first, had me falling to my knees. The hazy world around me began to speed up, the humans began to run faster, and more black shadows appeared. The screams got louder as the humans were attacked, and I grabbed my head and hunched forward until my forehead was touching the cold ground.

What is this?

"Ruby!"

That voice I didn't know. It was contorted, neither male nor female, but a mixture of many voices. It was the last thing I heard before I blacked out.

AXEL

They had been standing there for ten minutes before I noticed they were moving. First, it was Reika, when a small crease appeared between her brows. Then it was Natalie, with the way her hand had begun to twitch.

"Something's wrong," I said as I narrowed my eyes.

"They're fine," Olcan replied as he got up from his seat. However, he didn't approach them, and as I did, he held his hand up to stop me. "Small movements are nothing to worry about. We don't know what they are seeing."

Natalie and Reika's heads suddenly flung forward and then backward, their eyes wide open and as white as clouds.

"Is that normal?" Xavier yelled as he stepped forward, and Mathieu stood up as well.

"No," he said to Xavier as he placed his hand on his shoulder, "something's wrong."

Both women began shaking, and my heart skipped a beat as Ruby began to shake as well. "No fucking shit something's wrong! How do we stop it?" I ran forward, not waiting for someone's response. Just as I reached out to grab Reika's arm to pull her away from Ruby, Olcan grabbed me and pulled me back.

I didn't have time to be impressed by just how quickly he had gotten to me. I was more worried about Ruby and the way her eyes were now fluttering.

I flashed him off me. "If something is wrong, we need to pull them apart."

"If we force them apart, we will do them more harm than good. We might kill them."

I made a face and turned back to the shaking women. This was all new for me. My pack doesn't have an Enchanted, and while I've educated myself about them, there was still a lot I didn't know. My father never saw the need for an Enchanted.

"Mind links can be complex," Olcan said as he began circling them, his hands clasped behind his back. "Sometimes it's not just a link between minds. Right now Reika and Natalie aren't just seeing what's inside Ruby's mind, they are *in* her mind. Force them apart and their either their minds break or," He looked at me, and I clenched my fist at the smile on his face. "they die."

"And you're smiling because?" Xavier asked.

Olcan shrugged, "It's fascinating."

"Fascinating! Something is wrong with her!" I yelled, and Olcan arched a brow, that annoying smile on his lips still.

"So, you're worried about the human after all?"

My lips formed a thin line. "If she dies, if all three of them die right now, won't that be a problem?" He returned to his seat and sat down. There was no trace of concern or care in his eyes, not even for Reika. *What kind of man is this?* I turned away with my fingers rubbing my temples when I heard gasps.

I spun around as Reika and Natalie suddenly pulled away from Ruby as if she was the sun's surface. They both hunched forward, their hands on their heads as they began groaning in pain.

Mathieu grabbed Reika as Xavier made a dash for Natalie who looked dangerously close to fainting. Ruby was no longer shaking, but she was just standing there. I hated that my heart was racing, that I wanted to know if she was okay. When she finally started moving, I rushed forward. It was as if time was moving in slow motion as she began to sway and then fall. I reached out to her, her red hair covering her face as she fell when Xavier appeared and grabbed her just before she plummeted to the ground.

I watched him move her hair out of her face. She was saved from falling, so why was I so pissed all of a sudden? Why did I want to rip him limb from limb as he gently held her cheek and began calling her name?

"I-I don't understand," Reika said to herself as she held her head.

"What did you see?" Olcan asked, and she turned to stare at him. She looked like she had seen a ghost as she then looked down at Ruby in Xavier's arms.

"What is it?" I urged her on, and she shook her head and winced.

"She- I- I saw Elder Lovette," she whispered, and my eyes widened along with Olcan's and Mathieu. Olcan got to his feet slowly, his eyes flashing black as he looked at Ruby and then at Reika.

"Are you certain that..."

"Yes," Natalie replied as she lowered herself to the ground. "She's telling the truth."

Reika staggered and was caught again by Mathieu, her eyes becoming teary. This was not good, not good at all. If this was true, my problems weren't about to end, they were just beginning! "Why does a human have a memory of an Enchanted, of our Grand Elder Lovette?"

All eyes fell on Ruby because no one had an answer. I could see it in Xavier's eyes, the spark of doubt that I've felt for Ruby this whole time, and I sighed and left the room.

CHAPTER EIGHT
XAVIER

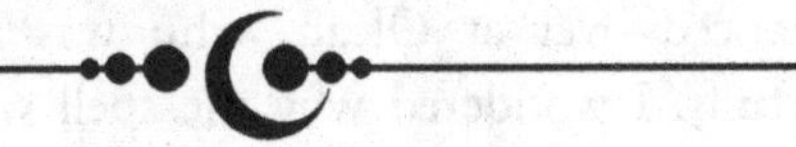

Reika released my hand while Axel removed his hand from her shoulder. I watched as a thin glowing string unwrapped itself from around my arm and Axel's and Ruby's as well. It vanished into thin air as she gently laid Ruby's hand on her stomach, her eyes still closed as she slept soundlessly.

It's been half an hour since she had fallen unconscious, and as the time stretched on, I became more and more anxious. Reika and Natalie had to be given the time to eat and replenish their strength. The rest of us - Olcan, my dad, Axel, and myself–have had to sit and wait to find out what had happened.

I spent the time trying to understand what Reika had meant about Ruby knowing one of the most well-known and beloved Enchanteds. My mind was straying and creating insane theories. There was one question that I just couldn't get out of my head: *what if Ruby really wasn't sent by our goddess?* What then? Was she truly my mate, or was this all some kind of elaborate spell or evil trick?

"Well?" Olcan asked, and Reika got to her feet rather shakily. Performing the spell she just did so soon after what happened with the mind link had severely weakened her. I turned and walked away once she was on her feet because my heart was in my throat waiting for what she might say in response.

"It's real," she whispered. "I can feel their bond. It's not a spell."

I glanced at Axel and found him already looking at me. If Natalie had known how to do this, or if we had even known this could be done, we would have done it from the start. It might have eliminated any reason for Axel to send word to the Council.

I glanced over at Olcan, who was now looking at Ruby thoughtfully. I wondered why the spell wasn't completed before Reika tried to see into her mind. Wouldn't it make more sense to find out if our bond was real to begin with? Because if it had been fake, it would've given Olcan and Axel the ammunition they needed. I suppose trying to invade Ruby's privacy came first on the Council's list of priorities. I shook my head. I suppose I had no right to be judgemental when I had forced Natalie to do the same thing once before.

"When will she wake up?" I asked as I turned around, and Reika shrugged.

"I don't know. What happened was extremely taxing on Natalie's body and mine, so just imagine what it might have been like for her. Forcing her awake isn't a good idea, so we'll just let her sleep."

My eyes darted to Olcan and caught the way he narrowed his eyes at her. Reika failed to notice because she was busy staring down at Ruby on the sofa. Natalie was sitting across the room with a cup in her hand as she stared out the window, her legs crossed lotus style.

"And what exactly happened just now?"

Reika looked Olcan's way before turning away to sit down. My dad entered the room at that moment and gave her a cup of tea before sitting down as well, a solemn expression on his face.

"You said you saw Lovette," he said as Reika blew on her tea, his baritone voice filling the room. "What exactly did you see?"

Natalie looked away from the window as the darkness outside started to be chased away by dawn, and Reika glanced her way for just a second. I frowned when I noticed how she held her forehead slightly to somewhat shield her eyes from Olcan while taking a sip of her tea. The look that passed between Nathalie and Reika was quick and all but imperceptible, but I was sure it meant something.

Despite my suspicions, I remained silent as she reclined in her chair and inhaled deeply. "Even with the two of us in there, we were only able to make a small crack. When you guys mentioned a wall in her mind, I had expected the normal defense mechanisms humans use to suppress memories. But there is an actual mental barrier within her mind. A strong one. And it was definitely made from magic." She closed her eyes and pinched the bridge of her nose. "I was only able to get a small glimpse of what is behind it and what I saw...who I saw, was Lovette." She opened her eyes and stared sternly at Olcan. "She was in tears, distraught about something, but that's all I saw before Ruby started to force us out."

Olcan made a sound of frustration. "How did she force you out? You're both strong Enchanteds. She's a frail human girl. So, we still know nothing and now have more questions than before. What will it take to break through?"

"A witch is needed for this, and a strong one. Powerful magic was used to create the block in her mind, and only powerful magic will be capable of bringing it down."

"I thought you Enchanteds were like witches," Axel said, and I had to stop myself from laughing. This is the future alpha of the Bluewater Pack? I had heard rumors that they didn't have an Enchanted among them, but I hadn't believed it. The Bluewater Pack has always been peculiar, right down to their practices and rituals. I could not deny that they've all been trained well, though, both from what I've heard and from fighting Axel myself.

"They are like witches, yes, but they have limits that witches do not," my father replied.

"I'll ask Willow to help," I said, but Olcan immediately shook his head. "No. The Council will find a witch," He got up and walked over to Ruby. He stood above her for a moment before walking away, his hands clasped behind his back. "How is it possible that she knew Lovette? It makes no sense."

Ruby groaned as her head turned from left to right. She raised a hand and held her forehead, and Natalie smoothly joined her on the sofa.

"Hey, take it easy," she said as she helped Ruby into a sitting position. "How do you feel?"

Ruby inhaled deeply, a deep crease between her brows as she looked around the room. "Like I was attacked by a wild animal," she said as she stared at Axel as if she suspected that he might have been that wild animal. He narrowed his eyes in response. "What's going on? What happened?"

"You forced Reika and me out of your mind, just like you did the first time I did a mind link with you."

"So, it didn't work then?" She asked weakly, and Natalie shook her head. She looked at Reika and frowned. "There is something, though, isn't there? What is it?" She looked my way. "What were you guys just talking about?"

"We saw something, yes," Reika replied, and Olcan crossed his arms over his chest.

If he was going to find a witch to break through the barrier in Ruby's mind, did it mean he was planning on staying here longer? Or would he force Ruby to leave with him? Neither of those options sat well with me, not with the way he kept staring at her as if he would happily open her skull himself to see what's inside. Ever since Reika had said what she had seen inside Ruby's mind, he'd become increasingly agitated.

My father cleared his throat and slid to the edge of his seat. "When I did my background check on you, Ruby, I found nothing about your parents and no record of where you actually came from. I just know that you were left at the hospital when you were born. If you know anything at all about where you're from, can you tell us now?"

"And no one thought that was odd and decided to press her for that information from the start?" Axel asked.

"That's not odd, Axel. Haven't you ever heard of an orphan? Believe it or not, I'm not the first human to grow up without their parents" Ruby snapped at him. "No, I don't know my parents or where I'm from. I was in and out of foster homes my entire life."

Olcan uncrossed his arms and buried his hands into his pockets. He tilted his head to the side like a curious dog. "Do you know a woman named Lovette?"

She looked thoughtful for a moment before shaking her head no. "I don't know anyone named Lovette. Why? Should I?"

"No. She's a Grand Elder for the Enchanteds. The same way wolves have a Council and Witches have High Priests and Priestesses, a Grand Elder is the most powerful of the Enchanteds. They often lead very sheltered lives because of this power." Ruby started to look confused, and my dad continued. "As I'm sure Natalie has told you, Enchanteds have lived with a lot of discrimination from other wolves for years due to the fact that they can never transform. However, there is something special about them that only a few outside of the Enchanted know - they are all descendants of our goddess."

"What?" Axel and I yelled in unison. I looked at Natalie and Reika for their reactions, but neither looked surprised at all. It's not like I doubted the existence of our goddess, but hearing something like this was blowing my mind. "Are you being serious right now?" I asked my father, and he nodded. "Why is something this important not widely known? So, you're telling me Natalie is related to our goddess?"

"Yes. The Council banned that information many years ago."

Axel hung his head and laughed. "Of course they did." He

pinned Olcan with a glare, "If other wolves found out there were actual descendants of our goddess living among us, they would demand the Enchanteds have a seat on the Council. Maybe they'd *be* the Council. Why listen to other wolves when we can listen to the children of the goddess that created us?" He shook his head. "But the power you Council members have would then be nothing compared to," he looked at Ruby and I was surprised to see awe within his eyes, "a demigod. Wolves deserve to know this."

"They will never deserve a seat on the Council," Olcan said through clenched teeth, his face turning slightly red. "Even though Enchanteds are wolves, they aren't pure wolves. They are a different species. The Council is for pureblood wolves only. That's why the Enchanteds formed their own faction. Enchanteds play an *amazing* and *honorable* role in our society, despite the fact that they aren't pure wolves. The Council has worked hard over the decades to stop the discrimination. Keeping this a secret isn't for the purposes of oppressing anyone. It is for the Enchanteds' own safety. Demigods invariably end up being used, abused, hunted, or killed for their powers. Why do you think demigods from other cultures are kept a secret or hidden? It's a sad fact that we cannot count on people's better natures to keep our precious resources safe."

"I'm sorry but what does all of this have to do with me?" Ruby asked, and Olcan turned to her, anger now in his eyes. I stepped closer to her.

Grand Elders worked closely with the Council, so I understood his anger and confusion. He had lost a friend when Lovette had disappeared. All wolves had grieved the loss.

"Lovette gave up her post as Grand Elder suddenly and vanished." His jaws clenched. "Her body was later found, and to this day, no one knows exactly what happened. All Enchanteds that show a strong connection to magic are appointed Grand Elder because they have the strongest connection to the Goddess. Because of this they don't...mingle, with anyone outside of the

Council or even their own people. Even under those circumstances, contact is limited. How do you, a human girl, with no people and no past, have a memory of our revered Lovette?"

Ruby frowned and looked away. "I-I don't know. I don't know anyone named Lovette."

"Do not lie to me!" Olcan roared. Mathieu swiftly got to his feet and placed himself between Ruby and Olcan. Axel and I stepped forward in unison as Olcan's breathing became labored, his eyes now black.

"Olcan, control yourself. You know she knows even less than we do." My dad said to him. "Yelling at her won't miraculously help her to remember things that were sealed away from even her."

Olcan took a deep breath and straightened his spine. Everyone watched as he cleared his throat and ran a hand down his shirt as he calmed himself. "I apologize for my outburst." He looked at Mathieu and then me. "It's clear Ruby isn't just an ordinary human girl after all, in more ways than just the fact that she is a human mated to two wolves."

He sideglanced at Axel, whose jaws clenched in response. I didn't trust either man, but Olcan even less so than Axel (and that was saying something). I had a bad feeling about how things were going to turn out forRuby with the addition of yet another unexplainable mystery. One that I, too, wanted answers to. Her knowing Lovette didn't have to mean something bad, but in what capacity could she have possibly come to know her? And why had Lovette been crying in the memory?

"So, Ruby met Lovette presumably sometime after she stepped down. Even so, correlation is not causation. Just because they had a relationship does not mean Ruby is the cause, directly or indirectly, of Lovette's demise.." I pointed out. Who knew my college Research Methods class would ever come in handy while trying to save my mate's life? Olcan's face twitched from the anger he was trying to contain. I could feel his dominance rolling through the room and poking at my flesh like needles. "You have no idea what the Grand Elder did after she left. You don't know everywhere she went and all the people she met." He didn't seem pleased to hear that, but he said nothing. He knew I had a point.

"If we knew everyone she had come into contact with after she left, everyone would be a suspect in her death until proven otherwise," Olcan said through clenched teeth, and Ruby got up and turned her back to everyone.

She stood there for a moment before stepping away, her face in her hands. Her hair was a tangled red curtain around her, and my finger twitched, yearning to feel one silky strand. If it wasn't for Axel'sgreed and his stupidity for involving the Council, Ruby and I would be so much closer now. Instead, I have to watch her deal with all of this from a distance.

I looked in Axel's direction where he rooted himself close to the door. I frowned because his eyes were glued to Ruby. They didn't hold the same indifference I've come to expect from him when it comes to her, and a stab of jealousy gripped my heart. Despite everything he's said, I know he's feeling the need to take her into his arms and protect her, the same way I am.

I don't think I'll ever be comfortable knowing that some part of her belongs to him. I can't help it; I want all of her to myself.

"Look, I'm sorry to hear that this Lovette person died. She was clearly important to all of you, and I would freely share with you anything I knew about her. The fact is, I just don't know anything about her. " She shrugged as she turned to face us, her eyes droopy and bloodshot from exhaustion and unshed tears. "I mean, maybe I do, but I can't remember. There is one thing I do know for sure, and that is that I sure as hell did not kill anyone. You came here to see if I'm really Axel and Xavier's mate, and I am." She said to Olcan and Reika before looking at Axel. "Xavier broke a law by saving my life and revealing to me that werewolves are real. So, what's going to happen now in terms of that?"

She looked Olcan's way once more. His face was now an unreadable blank canvas. "Those are the things you're here to clear up. Let's clear one thing up at a time, please, and tell me what's going to happen next. What's going to happen to me? Will I be spared because I'm a mate, or will I be killed because I'm a human that knows too much?"

No one spoke as they waited for Olcan's response. I sighed and looked away before walking to the window. The sun was now out and the world outside was bright and alive.

"I came here myself because I hadn't wanted this to get to any of the other Council member's ears. I wanted this issue resolved and put to sleep quietly." He made a soft chuckle as he pinched the bridge of his nose. "A human mate is unheard of, but here we are. Neither Axel nor Xavier will be forced to reject you because we don't know what effect that will have on you, or them, for that matter. You will be spared, Ruby, but now I have no choice now but to involve the other Council members. This is much bigger than it originally appeared to be. You will be coming back with Reika and me to Romania."

I felt like a cold hand had wrapped around my heart and was squeezing the life out of it the moment those words left Olcan's mouth. I glared at Axel, and I wished he could see the images in my mind of me ripping his fucking tongue out. Now, look at what he did! There will be no end to this any time soon, and Ruby is still in danger.

"I'm sorry, what?" Ruby announced as she stepped back, her eyes wide. "I'm not going to Romania. Fuck that! If I go anywhere with you, I don't need anyone to tell me that means my life is over. Whatever needs to be done will be..."

"Shut up!" Olcan yelled, and Ruby clenched her fists. I bit down on my tongue to stop myself from speaking, to hold back the urge to bite this man's throat out for speaking to my mate like that. The tension within the room was starting to become stifling, and Olcan closed his eyes and held his head back. "Know your place, human. Be grateful even being given this chance to live and come with us." He said calmly. "You don't have a choice in this matter, and neither does Xavier or Axel. They will both be coming with us as well. " He said this as he opened his eyes to stare at my dad, daring him to object. Despite the anger evident on my father's face, he remained silent. I love my father and have a lot of respect for him, but I hate how easily he rolls over sometimes.

"A witch is needed to get through whatever wall is in your mind. Hopefully, we will find out who created the wall in the first place, and that will all be done in Romania. You might have vital information about Lovette, so I can no longer keep this a secret from the others. You *will* be coming, and we *will* be leaving tomorrow. *All of us.* You all have one day to get your affairs in order."

He turned and left the room, and Ruby's wide teary eyes jumped from me to Axel and then back before she too ran from the room. Natalie sighed and leaned forward to palm her face, while Reika got up and left wordlessly. Axel remained standing by the door, but now he looked close to exploding. None of this had been t the outcome he had wanted. I had to admit, even though things were now fucked for everyone, I was secretly happy the smug prick was caught up in it, too. He made his bed, and now he was going to have to lie in it.

⸻ ••◆ ◆•• ⸻

RUBY

That bald fucking asshole wants to take me to Romania. Romania!

I kicked at a stone outside and watched as it bounced away from me. The only place I felt like I was alone was in the forest, although I knew, in reality, there were werewolves for miles around. I wasn't really alone, and it was clear I probably never would be again. Come to think of it, I still haven't received a tour to see any of the other houses. There was a whole community here, and all I'd seen so far was the main house and the training area. I guess that no longer matters. At this point, I'll be lucky to ever see this place again. I've been alone my whole life. There was always a part of me that had yearned for that to be different, but now with all this chaos and being constantly surrounded by people I wasn't sure if I could trust, I missed being alone. The fact was, I missed my old crappy life. As horrible as it had been, it was nothing close to this madness. Olcan had spared my life, but had he really? Dealing with one Council member had been bad enough. I just knew the moment I set foot into Romania, I'd have two other pompous asshole Council pricks gunning for me and whatever secrets I have hidden away in my mind. Once they find what they are looking for in my head, and once the story of Axel, Xavier and I start to spread, that'll become another whirlwind of problems. My impression of the Council is that anything that became too big of a problem to them tended to disappear conveniently. I was not excited to discover just how the Council intended to take care of me and all the problems I represented for them.

I sighed heavily and continued walking, the morning sun shining down through the gaps in the trees. As I hightailed it out of the house as fast as my legs could carry me, I had felt the intense urge to sob uncontrollably with all the anger and frustration that had built up over the course of the trial, but the moment I entered the woods I felt much calmer. Well, I wouldn't qualify it as calm exactly, but at least no longer on the verge of spontaneous combustion.

Birds and insects sang around me, but all I could hear were Olcan's words replaying in my mind.

I have no idea who this Lovette woman is...or was. And the more I thought about it, the more my head began to hurt. I stopped walking and held my head. My headache was becoming unbearable. It was at the point where I felt like it would be less painful to slam my head against a tree to just stop the overflow of thoughts, which continued to intensify the pain. *There are things from my past that I no longer know. There are people I've met; things I've said and done that I don't know. Am I who I even think I am?*

I felt like screaming.

The shadow of a bird above passed over the forest floor before me, its high-pitched cry echoing through the forest. I looked up in time to see brown wings before it vanished, and a tear finally slid down my cheek. I wish I could fly away from my life, from myself.

I have no idea who I am.

An image of what I had seen within my mind, of the running and screaming people, resurfaced, and more tears began to cascade down my cheeks. Was that a memory? It must have been, but what had happened? Who were those shadow people? Who took my memories from me?

"Fuck!" I screamed at the blue sky above, my body shaking. "Fuck!"

A twig snapped behind me, and I spun around and came face to face with a wolf, his black eyes narrowed with his massive tail swishing behind him. The last and only time I had seen Xavier in wolf form it had been night time, so now I could truly admire his size and beauty with the light of day. His paws were massive, his nails black and pointy. No one would mistake him for a normal wolf if they ever came across him. He was simply too massive.

He shook his body, and his fur ruffled somewhat. The jeans and shirt in his mouth swayed from side to side. He stepped forward, his paws digging into the ground as I dried my tears. I staggered back as he pushed his snout into my chest and dropped his clothes into my hand. His heavy breath fanned my face as he towered over me, and I giggled as he licked my cheek.

"Why do I need to carry them?"

He lowered his head for me to give him a head rub, and I closed my eyes as I gently pushed my fingers through his fur. He exhaled heavily before stepping away, and I opened my eyes as he started to circle me.

"What?" I asked and he stopped at my side and plopped down.

His black eyes blinked at me, and I shrugged. "What?" He shook his head and licked his shoulder before growling. "Do you want me to get on your back or something?"

He shook his head again and looked away as he angled his body more towards me. I made a face as I stared at him for a moment. *So, I'm about to ride a werewolf. Well, okay then.* I sniffled before tucking his clothes under my blouse, and he turned his head to look at me. I swallowed as I grabbed his fur, worried I might yank on it too hard, but after two tries I finally made it onto his back.

He got up suddenly, and I screamed, clenched my legs, and pressed myself to him. I've never ridden anything in my life, so it was hard to get past feeling like I could fall off of him any second. And it wasn't exactly a short distance to the ground. "Hey, hey, you're not wearing a saddle, sir. Please be careful." He shook his head and leaned forward, causing me to slide down closer to his neck. The ground was so far down. All I had was his fur to hold onto, which I didn't want to yank on too much for fear he might throw me off. "This was a bad idea."

He moved off, slowly this time, and I swallowed the lump that had lodged itself in my throat. I could feel the power in his body with each step he took, and I soon relaxed and leaned forward until I was lying on the back of his head. I could feel his heartbeat, strong and fast, and soon I closed my eyes before I realized it.

"Thank you," I whispered as the vibration from his heartbeat calmed my thoughts. He growled in response, and I smiled, when suddenly he jumped. I grabbed onto his fur and sat up to see what was happening, but he had only jumped over a log.

He started to walk faster. I gripped his fur and lowered myself the way I've seen people do while riding a horse. He slowly began to pick up the pace until he set off on a run. At first, I panicked, scared that I would be thrown off him, but soon the wind in my hair, his heartbeat beneath me, and the freedom I felt had me laughing and urging him on.

We zoomed through the trees, leaving the house, the pack, and my mysterious past behind. If I could freeze time and create an endless loop, this would be the moment I would choose to repeat. I could be free forever with Xavier.

He slowed down until he was walking again, and I frowned as the sound of water met my ears. I was panting as if I was the one that had been running as I looked around, and soon a waterfall came into view. My eyes widened and excitement set in as he crunched down and I slid off him. We walked together down a small hill down to the waterfall, and I placed his clothes on a rock as I walked forward to see the falls and pond surrounded by vibrant bright flowers and full bushes. It was like an oasis in the middle of the forest, This was what I needed.

I scratched him behind his ear, a face splitting smile on my face. "Thank you."

He made a sound and walked forward into the pond. I watched as he dove in, and I waited as seconds went by and he didn't resurface. I frowned and began removing my clothes.

"Xavier?" I called as I entered the pond. I closed my eyes for a moment as I bent down to scoop up the cool water. "Xavier? Stop messing around. You're a wolf, not a merman."

Something brushed against my leg and instead of screaming in surprise like I'm sure he had intended , I dived in to grab him. We resurfaced together, his arms around my waist.

"Well, look at you, trying to be a badass. I could have been a piranha or something. "

"Or something," I replied as I wrapped my hands around his neck. The smile on my face fell as I stared at the falls behind him. "Too bad you're showing me this now when we'll be leaving tomorrow."

He released me and moved a strand of hair that was stuck to my face before pushing off, "Don't think about any of that right now, Ruby. Right now, nothing else matters. After today, whenever you feel down, you will always have this memory to think back to. "

And I know I have a lot of sad days ahead. "On the upside, you'll be there with me."

"So will Axel," he added before he submerged himself and reappeared again. He combed his hair back and swam to me. "Although I'd rather him not be there at all, he needs to be there for you."

I frowned. "Be there for me? You'll be there for me. He's the one responsible for bringing in the Council, to begin with, which is the only reason we have to go at all. Everything is going sideways thanks to him."

"When it comes to blaming Axel, I'm happy to be first in line, but I don't think we can lay this completely on him. I think this would have all happened eventually, to be honest. You have some kind of connection to a Grand Elder. I don't think that would have stayed buried forever. I think it has to mean something."

I sank lower into the water until my chin was covered. "You're right, let's not talk about any of this." I swam away from him towards the falls and took a deep breath as I dived under.

I came out on the other side of the falls where there was a dip in the rocks, almost like a little cave. I climbed onto the rock and sat down, and soon Xavier popped up out of the water.

He nestled his way between my legs, and I couldn't stop myself from combing his hair back, the wet strands gliding through my fingers. "Can I ask you something?"

He nodded lazily, "Sure, as long as you keep doing that."

"Are mermaids real?"

He pulled back, his lips curving into a smile. "Seriously?"

I shrugged as I laughed. 'What? I wanna know."

He nodded, and my eyes widened. "But they aren't gorgeous women with long hair and seashells for a bra." He reached up and moved my hand from his hair to kiss my palm, and the action sent a burst of electricity up my arm. "I'll take you to meet one someday."

"Angels?"

"Yes, they're real," He replied as he kissed my wrist.

"Demons?"

He nodded as he kissed the dip at my elbow, and my toes inadvertently curled under the waterline. My lips parted to ask him another question, but he pressed his lips to mine before I could. I swallowed my words and my eyes fluttered closed as I wrapped my legs and arms around him.

He gripped my waist and pulled me closer as his tongue explored my mouth, and I moaned into his. I had missed him so much. The sky could open up at this very moment to rain meteorites down on the earth, and I wouldn't let him go.

He pulled away and pressed his lips to my cheek and then my neck. "I missed you," he whispered. I sighed and pressed myself to him even more, his words music to my ears. "Even if Olcan hadn't *ordered* me to go to Romania as well, I'd still find my way there just to be with you." He pulled away to stare into my eyes, and I pouted as sadness set into my heart once more. "I'm not letting you out of my sight again, Ruby, and I don't care if you get tired of me."

I shook my head. "I'll never get tired of you. But Xavier, no one knows what's in my head, what's in my past. I don't..."

"Nothing from your past will ever change how I feel about you. We're in this together."

CHAPTER NINE
RUBY

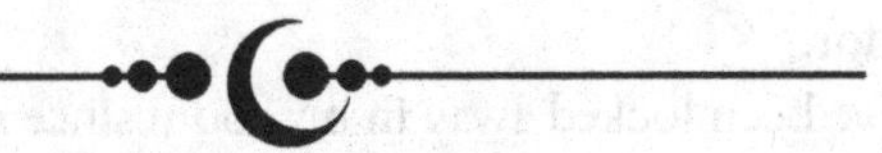

I could still feel Xavier's lips on me and his strong hands holding me, even hours later. Amid this chaos, he had made me forget everything so easily even if it had only lasted for a few hours. I had needed the distraction, a break to experience some form of normalcy. I know now that, if given the choice to go back and time make different choices that would allow me to live my life as I had been, I would still make the same choices again. That might be the selfish thing to do, but I'd still want to know Xavier, Natalie, and Mathieu. I'd still want to know about werewolves and witches.

I paused as I looked from left to right, my mouth twerked to the side in contemplation. I'm not sure I'd want to meet Axel. That prick has single-handedly ruined everything. Well, at least now he's been pulled into the madness against his will, which he deserves, of course. I don't get how he thought he could walk away from this unscathed. This is just further proof of what I've thought all along - karma's a bitch.

One thing I did fear was the idea that perhaps Xavier might come to resent me one day for all the trouble I have caused him and his pack. Yes, he wasn't feeling that way now and professed to be ready to leave his pack for good to be with me, but the trouble certainly wasn't over yet by any means. Axel has proved he's ready to reject me or pawn me away for his pack. Was it only a matter of time before Xavier came to feel the same?.

Will he eventually hate me because he picked me over being something he was born to be? Maybe he'll learn to hate me long before that because no one knows what's in my past. I shook my head to be rid of those thoughts and continued walking down the corridor.

I've been locked away in my room since returning to the house with Xavier, a different room than the one I had been sharing with Axel. I didn't want to see or speak to anyone, and the last person I wanted to run into was Olcan. I had only eaten when Natalie had turned up with dinner. She had finally filled me in on how an Enchanted named Adolfa had transferred all her power to her and the significance of her hair color change.

I was still blown away by the fact that she's a descendant of a goddess, a real goddess. It had been hard to follow everything that Olcan and the others were talking about this morning, but that bit of information had been mind-blowing. I hated the fact that I would be leaving her behind, but at the same time, I was happy she wouldn't have to be dragged to another country as well on account of me.

Considering it was already 10 pm and we all had a dreaded day ahead of us tomorrow, everyone had retired to their own spaces early. This was the perfect time for me to roam around or whip something up in the kitchen. It really wasn't hunger driving me to leave my room.I was just too anxious to stay in one place any longer, and I was eager to stretch my legs. I wanted to take one last long look at this place. Despite everything I've been through here, this was the best home I have ever lived in. I hoped my socks were allowing me to move around without being heard and that was proved to be accurate when I walked by a slightly cracked door and heard Axel talking.

"This isn't what we agreed on."

I frowned and pressed myself to the wall beside the door before peeping inside. Sure enough, Axel was standing with his back to the door, his hair loose around his shoulders. I couldn't see whom he was speaking to, but I had a strong suspicion about who it might be.

"Plans change," I heard Olcan respond in his usual indifferent tone, and I edged closer to the door.

"My father has been ill for a while, and I've already taken over as Alpha. You know that."

This was news to me and I had a feeling it would be news to Xavier as well. I pressed myself closer to the wall instead of looking into the room and risking being seen. Did they know I was standing here? Surely, they could smell me, or were they too engrossed in their conversation to notice?

"I can't leave my pack and go to Romania. Can you even say how long I'll have to stay there? No, you have no idea."

Olcan sighed. "This isn't up for debate, Axel. I think it's obvious that you can't be left behind. You are the girl's mate as well. Your presence will be needed."

"This *is* up for debate. This is not the deal we made. This is a bad time for me to leave my people," Axel growled.

"Deals change! A lot has changed! This was a bad time for me to drop everything to come here, but here I am. She is a problem, Axel, much more than you had portrayed, and more than any of us had thought."

"Because she knows Lovette? This is how she is treated because of that? You don't know what she knows."

"Exactly!" Olcan yelled. "No one knows what she knows! No one knows who she is!" My eyes fluttered as I looked down, his words cutting through me. "I need to know what she knows, everything that she knows." His voice grew deep and threatening, and I clenched my fists, my nails digging into my palms. "And I will learn it all, even if I have to cut it from her skull myself. I don't give a fuck about her being your mate or Xavier's. She's not one of us, and she never will be. You're both alphas-to-be. In fact, you're already an acting alpha, so act like it."

Was Olcan saying what I thought he was saying? Was he talking about killing me? He couldn't be. *No.* My heartbeat spiked as I continued to listen, but they were no longer speaking. As the silence stretched on, I started to panic that maybe they had finally realized I was eavesdropping right outside the door. I had just started to move away when Axel's voice met my ears, his voice as low as Olcan's.

"What are you saying, Olcan?"

"Don't tell me that now after all this you actually care about what happens to her, Axel. I'm here because you brought me here. Xavier is already too close to her and that will be taken care of, but don't you join him, Axel. You'll meet the same fate, and I don't want to lose yet another promising Alpha, especially one who understands the Council's vision. A human can't be mated to a wolf. Period. Imagine the chaos and uncertainty within the wolf community if something like this ever got out. We must understand how this happened and how to prevent it from happening again."

I turned away slowly on tiptoe until I felt like I was far enough away from the room. Then I started running. *I have to get out of here. I can't stay here. I can't!* I ran down the stairs to get to the second floor but as I rounded a corner, I heard whispering. I stopped running, my chest rising and falling rapidly as I listened, but the whispering had stopped.

I started walking down the dimly lit hall, the hairs on the back of my neck standing on end as the faint whispering started once more. I spun around in time to see a black shadow disappear inside the wall to my left. My eyes widened as I immediately turned and started running. Ghost or not, I wasn't sticking around to find out.

I pumped my legs as the feeling of being chased grew worse. I heard a scream, much like the ones I had heard during that vision inside my mind. I skidded to a halt as the world around me fell away, and I was once again at that place in my mind with all the humans running in fear.

I rubbed at my eyes, and when I opened them, I was in the hall once more.

What the hell is going on?

"Ruby?" The voice hadn't registered until I had spun around and my fist was caught inches away from crushing a nose. Xavier's head tilted to the side; his brows knitted as he lowered my fist. "What are you doing?" I threw myself at him and buried my face in his chest. "Ruby, you're freaking me out. Why were you running like that?"

"Something was..." I looked up at him. "We have to leave, Xavier."

He stared down at me sadly. "We have to go, Ruby. We don't have a choice."

I untangled myself from him as I shook my head. He had no idea what was about to happen. "They're going to kill me." His expression of pity didn't change, and I felt like punching him in the face for real. "I'm not being paranoid, Xavier. I heard Olcan say it aloud. He's going to kill me. I don't know exactly what he has planned for you, but I doubt it'll be pleasant."

His face slowly morphed into one of confusion and anger. "What are you talking about? You heard Olcan talking when? To whom?"

"Just now, on the third floor, he was talking to Axel. He wants to know what I know, and he's prepared to do anything to get that information. He said I'm not one of you and I never will be. , He doesn't care that I'm mated to you and Axel. All he wants to find out is how I'm mated to a wolf, to begin with, and how to stop it from happening again. He has no plans of ever letting any wolves get a whiff about our mate bond. He's going to kill me, Xavier. We have to leave now."

He stepped away from me, his face turning red with rage. With his black T-shirt and jeans and the semi-darkness around us, he blended into the shadows around us easily while pacing back and forth. "Axel's the Alpha now because his dad is sick," I said, and as I expected, he turned to me with confusion written on his face. Obviously that was news to him, too. "He's mad about being forced to leave his pack behind to come with us, but Olcan doesn't care about that either. He doesn't care about any of us."

"She's right."

Xavier looked over his shoulder to find Natalie standing in the shadows a few steps away from us. She walked forward and into the light, her hands buried in the pockets of her leather jacket.

"Olcan doesn't care about any of us, but especially not Ruby," she said as she came to a stop beside Xavier. "He cares about control, and this is quickly becoming something that's out of his control. You both need to leave."

"That's easier said than done, Natalie, and you know that. Today is a full moon, or had you forgotten? That means I can't shift if we run into trouble. We'll be sitting ducks if we're caught. " he replied. "When Olcan catches us, then we'll absolutely be screwed, and that might even extend to the whole pack."

"We can't stay here, either," I said to him, and he sighed and pressed a finger to his temple. "There has to be something we can do."

"There is," Natalie replied, and Xavier and I looked at her as she turned her back to us. "There is a way you can both leave without Olcan noticing. Just leave it up to me. I'll cover things here, but be packed and ready to leave in a few hours."

"Are you sure?" Xavier questioned, and she turned around to face us once more. Her eyes were glossy, and it tugged at my heart because it was clear this was all painful for her. She nodded before walking over to him and hugging him. "But you and dad…"

"Will be fine," she said to him as she stepped away. "You and

Ruby need to stay *together*, no matter what." She looked at us both sternly, and we nodded.

She pulled me in for a hug as well, and my eyes began to fill with impending tears. I felt like I was stuck in a nightmare that kept going from bad to worse instead of me waking up to find out it was all a bad dream. "Pack and be ready by midnight. Just meet each other outside and leave. I'll take care of everything. Always remember that I love you both. Trust no one, and try not to worry. I can always find you both at any time and do a mind link. We'll stay in touch."

She turned away and vanished into the shadows down the hall. "Where will we go?" I asked, and Xavier pulled me to him and kissed the top of my head. My heart was beating so fast I felt like I could faint any minute. "I- I..." I wanted to be strong for him, I wanted to be brave when I needed to be, but the reality was I terrified. I felt betrayed that Axel had conspired with Olcan in planning to kill me, but I'd never say it. I thought that he felt enough of the bond to keep him from wanting to end my life, but I guess I had given him more credit than he deserved. Apparently, he is just like Olcan - all he cares about is power. "I want this all to end."

He pulled back and kissed me gently on the lips. "It will, but first we need to do this."

"Will you tell your dad?"

Pain flashed within his eyes, and he shook his head. "I can't risk him trying to stop me and I'd rather that he have plausible deniability about being involved when Olcan realizes we've left. Get packed. I'll see you soon."

●—————●● ●●●

NATALIE

I had to change my sheets after waking up. They were damp with my sweat, and even my hair was wet. I looked as if I had taken a dip in a pool. Like so many things in the supernatural world, astral projection was definitely not as easy as they made it seem in movies or on TV. After taking a shower, I went looking for Ruby. I didn't bother going to her room. I already knew she wasn't there.

Now that they both know what Olcan is up to and are ready to leave, everything is about to fall apart...as it must.

I felt like punching something as I made my way back to my room. Things were already set into motion, and there would be no going back.

I rounded the corner to get to my room and spotted Reika standing by the door. Her eyes remained on me until I stopped before her, my arms crossed over my chest.

"Did you tell them to go?" I heard her ask in my mind, and I nodded.

"Yes," I replied telepathically, and she stepped aside for me to open my room door. She followed me inside, and I crossed the room to sit by my window. "I told them to leave. They're getting ready now."

I previously had no idea Enchanteds could communicate telepathically, but now I had Reika to thank for bestowing that particular piece of useful knowledge. I stared up at the moon hanging low in the sky and a chill passed over my body as Reika pulled up beside me to stare up at the sky as well.

"Do you think Axel will follow them?" She asked me. Her voice in my mind sounded as clear as if she was physically speaking.

"He will," I replied. "No matter how much he tries to act indifferent towards Ruby, the connection he has with her is there. He won't be able to stay away. The more time he spends around her, the stronger the connection grows. So no matter how little he wants to, wherever they go, he'll follow. He might have started some of this all out of selfishness, but he was also trying to be a good alpha, to give his people better lives and a better home to run free. Wolves need space. Now he has learned the real truth about the Council." I shook my head. "They are all the same, selfish, power-hungry leeches." I looked over at her. "No offense."

She shrugged. "None taken, I merely work for Olcan in matters like this when an Enchanted is needed. At first, I, too, was blind to the Council's true nature. Yet, even after I figured it out, I stayed."

"Why? You could have left and joined a pack."

Her mouth turned downward. "I could have, but to be blunt, I didn't have the courage to. I turned a blind eye to their corruption like so many others do in order to ensure my own survival. Because I'm pretty sure my life would have been forfeit if I left. The Council doesn't hesitate to put a target on the back of anyone they consider to be a threat. I know too much. " I walked over to my bed and sat down while she remained at the window, her head still held back as she stared up at the sky. "I love the full moon. It is the only time the other wolves experience what it's like to be us." She said, and her chuckle echoed loudly in my mind. "I'd never trade what I am to be like them. All of what Olcan had said about Enchanteds playing an honorable role in our society was bullshit. We're used and looked down on not because we are "precious resources" to them, but because they are jealous and afraid of our power. So what if we can't change into hairy beasts? We are the goddess's children. Yet we still live under the thumb of their oppression.."

"Not for much longer," I replied, and she looked my way. I could see the questions within her eyes, and I quickly looked away. "Are you sure you'll be able to do what you need to do tonight? Without you putting Olcan and Mathieu into a deep sleep, Xavier and Ruby will be caught."

"I'll get it done, Natalie. Just trust me."

We didn't speak for a while, my mind taking me elsewhere until Reika crossed the room to sit on the bed beside me. The burning behind my eyes grew worse, and I looked away. Xavier has always been like a brother to me and I've grown close to Ruby. It killed me that there wasn't much more I could do to help them, to prepare them for what was to come.

"I wish there was something more I could do. Something I could tell them to warn them. I wish I could warn everyone, but I can't. Even if I wanted to, I couldn't. I'm bonded by oath. If I interfere with what's to happen, it'll only be worse."

"They'll be okay, Natalie," she whispered in my mind again as she took my hand and squeezed it gently. A tear fell from my eye, and I quickly swatted at it.

"If only you knew what I do."

"That's because you refuse to tell me everything," I said nothing in response and pinned her with a look. "But, *but,* I know you can't. You joining that mind link and showing me what had happened with Adolfa, what had happened to you...that was something. I'm just thankful you trusted me enough to show me. I've only ever heard rumors about power transfer. To suspect in theory that an Enchanted can pass on her gifts to another is one thing, but to have seen it done with my own eyes is something else. It must have been excruciating. , I suppose the Council is responsible for suppressing information about Enchanted power transfers as well."

Of course, they wouldn't want something like that to get out. Enchanteds would surely become too powerful if they found out they could take on the powers of another. A loved one that has become too old and was ready to die would pass on their skills to the younger generation. I could see where we would push the boundaries of mortality. I could see the many Enchanteds lives that could be lost if the practice was misused. Not all wolves are like the Council members, and not all Enchantedshave good intentions. It would be chaos. Despite my dislike for the Council, I actually couldn't fault them for keeping this a closely guarded secret. "It was excruciating, and a life was lost. Yet, for what's coming, it was completely necessary, and a small price to pay. We are all going to need as much strength as possible for what's to come."

"Who is Ruby?" The question caught me off guard, and I pulled my hand away from hers. She turned to face me. "Did she truly know Lovette?"

"She did. You saw that she did." I got up and walked away before turning to face her. "Reika, there are things that I don't know. In fact, there is a lot I don't' know. My job is to keep Xavier, Ruby, and Axel on the right path. That is all."

She didn't respond and got up. "I understand." Her voice echoed in my mind as she walked to the door. "It's time for me to do what I need to do."

She left, and I returned to my bed, this time plopping down face forward. Despite the full moon and the light, it was blessing the earth with tonight is the beginning of dark times. I'd be setting Xavier, Ruby, and Axel on their path tonight for better or worse, and my job would come to an end. Unfortunately, that will not erase what I know. and That burden I will have to carry with me to the end.

I got up and ran my hand down my clothes. There was one last thing for me to do while Reika performed the sleeping spell on Olcan and Mathieu.

I walked to the center of the room and closed my eyes, and when I reopened them, I knew they were no longer my typical shade of blue but instead, a milky white. I waved my hand, and what looked like a shimmering sheet of light began to crawl over the walls. Once the room was sealed, I walked over to my closet and removed a small rectangular box from under a pile of clothes.

I sighed as I stared down at the wooden box, strange writings engraved on it that only I could see. "I hate this part. I really hate this part."

I returned to the middle of the room and sat on the floor. I placed the box in front of me and exhaled as I closed my eyes, fear gripping me in a tight embrace. I knew what I had to do. I didn't have a choice. I listened to my breathing for a moment before opening my eyes and repeating the words written on the box.

As my chanting grew louder, the words began to glow, one letter at a time. Once all the letters were glowing, I opened the box to reveal a silver dagger. I swallowed as I picked it up and turned it over in my hand. If anyone was watching, they would think I had maybe removed a spell from the box. In fact, I actually summoned this dagger from somewhere else, another plane to be exact.

The double-bladed dagger was warm to the touch. I held its' crystal-encrusted handle with both hands and closed my eyes. I didn't give myself time to think before I plunged the dagger into my chest.

My body stiffened instantly and, my eyes grew wide from the pain that was burning through my chest. I felt my life force draining away, and my head fell back as I started to scream. Tears began to flow from my eyes, but instead of falling downward, they started to float above me. Suddenly, my head was thrown forward.

I could hear whispering voices, and a chill went through my body.

"Yes, I can hear you." I didn't recognize my own voice as it was deep and contorted. I sounded possessed. I tightened my hold on the blade handle, blood soaking through my blouse. "I did as you asked." The whispers echoed through the room, and my head bent to the side. "Yes, I know, but I had no choice." My head bent to the other side, and I sighed. "I understand." I listened to the whispers, to my new instructions, and my body jerked as I felt the feathery touches of a hand caress my cheek. "But there has to be some way to…" The whispers grew loud, and I winced, more tears leaving my eyes to hover above me. "Okay, I understand."

The dagger in my chest vanished, and my hands fell to my sides. I gasped as I fell forward and then started to cough as air filled my lungs. The pain in my chest was gone, as if stabbing myself had just been a bad dream, but my body was shaking uncontrollably. I pressed my cheek to the cold ground as the images before my eyes started to clear, and I knew my eyes had now returned to their normal color.

I laid there for a moment, my energy completely depleted. The pain I had felt as I thrusted that dagger into my chest was nothing compared to what I had just seen.

I'm not sure exactly when I dozed off, but when I woke up, I was lying on my back, dried tears on my cheeks making my skin feel stiff. I felt strong enough to get up, so I made my way to the bathroom. I removed my bloody top and touched a finger to my chest. There wasn't even a scar.

I'm glad that was the first and last time I'd have to do something like that. I felt like I had been hit by a bus. I soaped up my rag and began scrubbing at the dried blood on me. The water was scorching hot, but I barely felt it. I was too lost in my thoughts.

Had I really just killed myself?

"Natalie?"

My hand froze where I had been washing my legs, and I stood up straight.

"Yes? Did you do it?" I asked Reika through our mind link.

"I did. They're asleep, and neither will wake until the morning."

I turned the tap on full blast and stepped under it. "Good. Now all they need to do is survive."

CHAPTER TEN
RUBY

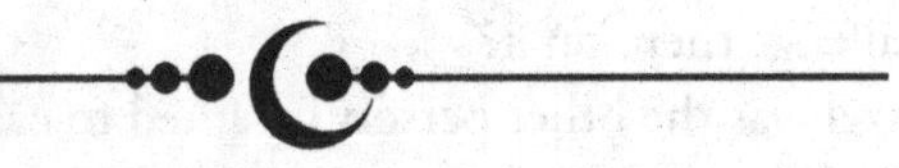

I packed immediately after getting to my room and stashed the backpack under my bed. I had a suitcase packed and placed by the door just in case Olcan decided to stop by and check up on me. He'd see that I was ready to leave. I just wouldn't be leaving with him.

All that was left to do was for me to wait until midnight to meet Xavier outside, but waiting was harder than I thought it would be. I spent the time pacing back and forth in my room until I got paranoid that someone might hear me moving around and wonder why I was so excessively active late at night.

I laid on my bed after that, twisting and turning until I settled on facing the window. With the moon's light shining down, it appeared unusually bright outside. While it looked beautiful, I was worried. Xavier wouldn't be able to shift tonight, which made both of us vulnerable. I know he would still be incredibly strong, but nowhere near his best.

Natalie said she would take care of everything, whatever that meant. I was trying to put my faith in her and not worry. That is really hard to do when you are used to something always going wrong. That was my childhood in a nutshell, and my young adulthood wasn't shaping up to be any better so far, that's for sure. I wasn't sure why it was still surprising to me that Olcan wanted me dead. I had no doubt going to Romania wouldn't have been a vacation but being killed wasn't in my plans. Considering that Reika had confirmed for him that the mate bond was real and mates are protected by law...but hey, who am I kidding? The Council were the ones making all the rules. They can change them, or even break them, as they see fit. Who would even know about it to challenge them on it?

Axel was the other person I wanted to castrate. Why wasn't he tearing Olcan a new one for talking about killing me! That's another thing I should stop being surprised about. Axel isn't Xavier, and he'll never be Xavier. I might be mated to him, but the connection is barely there. The only time I had even felt something towards him was during our drive here when he had opened up to me about wanting to be a good alpha. He was like a parent that would do anything to provide for his kids, and that at least I could understand. Conspiring with Olcan was something I couldn't, wouldn't forgive him for.

The hours went by agonizingly slow, but eventually, I was standing in front of my door with my backpack on. My hair was wrapped into a bun, and I pulled my hoody over my head while I zipped my sweater to my throat. Not for the first time tonight, I wished Xavier could shift. I'm sure we could cover more ground with me riding him.

I reached out and held the door handle, my hand shaking as I opened it slowly. I didn't make a sound, but I continued to move slowly, opening it just enough to slip through and taking my time to close it quietly once more.

Whatever Natalie planned to do, I hoped she had already done it. I wasn't about to go running through the house to test it out. I was sure it took twenty minutes at least to make it outside. When I finally did, my heart was pounding out of my chest. I gratefully inhaled the cool night air.

A shadow appeared from behind a tree at the forest line, and my heart skipped a beat until the shadow waved at me. I narrowed my eyes and when I realized it was Xavier, I dashed towards him. I threw myself into his arms, and he kissed the top of my head before taking my hand and leading me into the forest.

"We made it out," I whispered to him as he stared at the house. I bit my lip as the muscles in his jaws clenched. He threw his hood over his head and turned. "Are you okay?" I knew I was a stupid question to ask. He was about to run away from his home, his father, and his pack. I just didn't know what else to say.

"I will be, once we get far away from here."

He took my hand, and we started walking briskly. We stopped from time to time for him to listen to the forest. Even though his hearing was ten times better than mine would ever be, his heightened abilities weren't at their usual level because of the full moon. We were still in his pack's territory and running into another wolf wouldn't be good. With our backpacks on our backs, it was clear that we were running away and not just going out for a late-night stroll.

"I wonder what Natalie had to do to 'take care of things'," he said as he avoided walking in a pocket of moonlight beaming down through the canopy of trees above.

"Why?"

"We made it out and made it this far. Council members are like royalty, which means they are stronger than even alphas. Their senses are heightened to the max, so I'd expected old Olcan to be on high alert tonight. He'd be the first hear when someone so much as coughed in bed, much less when two people got up and left the house."

I moved a tree branch from before my face. "Natalie's different, stronger. Whatever she did, it worked." Despite how briskly we were walking, I knew he felt like we were moving too slowly. He was going at this pace just so I could keep up. "Have you ever met any of the other Council members?" I asked as I picked up the pace to show him that I could go faster. Yes, I was tired, but knowing what I was running from was motivation enough to keep me going.

"No. Olcan's the first Council member I've met. Council members don't usually make appearances like this. They send representatives."

I didn't respond, and we kept walking until Xavier suddenly stopped. "What?" I asked, and he pressed a finger to my lips.

He pointed his head to the sky and inhaled asI started looking around us. Despite the moonlight, the forest was still too dark for me to see much. I wanted to ask him what he was hearing or smelling in the air but kept my mouth shut. I had grabbed a knife on my way out of the house, and I removed it slowly from where it was tucked into my left sleeve as Xavier turned his back to me and positioned himself protectively in between whatever he sensed and me.

"Come out. I can smell you," he growled, and my heart fell to my feet.

Fuck, they caught us!

I remained behind Xavier when I heard leaves crunching under feet. *Hell, noo, I'm not going back, not without a fight!* I stepped out from behind him, my knife in hand.

"Axel?" I looked him up and down with my knife still raised, and he looked down at the blade reflecting the moon's light. His eyes flicked up to mine and the corner of his mouth arched a little before Xavier growled and it fell away. They stared at each other for a moment and Axel rubbed at his nostrils and shook his head.

So Olcan sent him after us. How theatrical.

"Did you really think I couldn't smell you standing outside the door?" He asked before his eyes slid to me once more, and I glared at him.

"So, you knew I could hear you talking to Olcan about killing me? Yeah, that makes me feel so much better. I get the message,

Axel, you care that little about me." I widened my stance. "I'm not going to Romania."

He shrugged. "Good. I'm glad. "

"What?" I asked, shocked at his response.

"Why are you following us?" Xavier added, and I finally noticed the backpack Axel was carrying.

"None of this was what I wanted," he said, and I scoffed.

"Yeah, you just wanted to get rid of the Blackmoon Pack," I snapped at him, and to my surprise, he nodded. *This man clearly has no shame.*

"Yes, I wanted to get rid of the Blackmoon Pack, but not like this. All I've wanted is to be allowed back onto this land. It's big enough for both packs to co-exist comfortably. All I've ever wanted is a better existence for my pack."

"Yeah, I heard you're Alpha now," Xavier replied, a growl in his voice. "What's wrong with your father?"

Axel's face morphed into one of anger. The last thing that needed to happen right was another fight between these two. "That's not important right now, is it? I'm not here to take you guys back, okay. I'm coming with you."

Xavier laughed, and I lowered my knife. Axel, however, remained serious as he waited for Xavier to realize he wasn't kidding. *He wants to come with us? Why? He started all of this because of his duty to his pack, and now he is ready all of a sudden to make himself a fugitive and leave them behind?* Yeah, I didn't believe him either.

"We don't need you to come with us, Axel. I think you've done enough. So, you want me to believe that you're suddenly willing to leave your pack to follow us? The Council will be coming after us and you."

"I don't blame either of you for not trusting me, but believe it or not, I'm on your side." I laughed. and he stepped forward. Xavier immediately held his hand out to block me. Axel stepped back, despite the growl that had left his lips. "I'm already on the

Council's radar now, and my pack will be as well if I return to them."

Neither Xavier nor I said anything, and he sighed and held his forehead. This was the most words I've ever heard from his lips. If he was acting, he deserved an Oscar.

"Trust me if you want to, or don't. but I'm on your side. No matter what you both think, I don't want to see you die, Ruby. None of the three of us asked for this, but this is apparently how it is going to be. Fighting it, and each other is only making all of our lives worse."

Xavier's hand dropped after blocking me to adjust the strap of his bag on his shoulder. I couldn't tell if he was buying what Axel was selling, but I was (despite my better judgment). Maybe I'm stupid, but why would Olcan send him and only him to take us back? Then again, it's not like he could send Reika or Mathieu. I felt torn. It bothered me that I was so easily trying to find reasons to give him the benefit of the doubt, considering that this entire mess was his fault. As I went over the conversation between Axel and Olcan in my mind again, I realized I never actually heard Axel agree to my death. In retrospect, I realized, if anything, he had sounded surprised that Olcan had said it.

"Look, Ruby, you are my mate. I'm not good at this kind of stuff. I still have my doubts because you know a Grand Elderand it changes a lot." He turned to Xavier. "Olcan wants what's inside her head and if he gets it, he's going to kill her and everyone that knew about her. We are wasting time standing here and debating this. Besides, the Council will be hunting you guys. If that's the case, the way I see it, you need all the help you can get."

"Okay," Xavier replied, and I frowned. I stared at him, surprised he was agreeing. Axel removed his bag from one shoulder and swung it around him to open it.

"What? Are you serious?" I whispered to Xavier, although I knew Axel could hear me just fine. "*Okay*? Just like that?'

"He's right. If the Council gets their hands on you, we're all dead—my dad, Natalie, everyone. With Axel with us, he'll be able to protect you as well. That doesn't mean I automatically trust him. Believe me, I will be watching him." He said that bit loudly, but Axel only kept searching through his bag.

"Here," Axel said as he approached us, three small vials of slightly brownish liquid in his hand. "I had these created by witches for my pack. It masks a wolf's scent. I was able to track you guys all too easily."

"I'm not drinking that. You said it is for wolves." I pointed out as I crossed my arms. This could be some kind of trick - maybe a sedative that would put Xavier and me to sleep.

"It masks anyone's scent. You were given it when you were taken." He took one of the vials, popped it open and drank it. "See? Make no mistake, by morning they'll be hunting us so our scents need to stop here."

I didn't feel comfortable doing this, but what other choice did I have? We had wasted too much time standing here chatting as it was. Xavier and I each took a vial and chugged it. Let me tell you, the taste was utterly repellent, but within seconds, Xavier pointed out that he could no longer smell me or Axel.

We walked on in uncomfortable silence, and I remained close to Xavier's side while Axel followed behind us. After an hour passed, exhaustion began to set in. My legs were dragging and I was slowing down, despite my initial resolve to keep up. Axel and Xavier were still maintaining at the same brisk pace they had set throughout the journey with no outward signs of fatigue that I could see.

"I'm exhausted," I said, and Xavier took my backpack. The weight off my shoulders was a relief, but my legs were still killing me.

"Where are we going anyway?" Axel asked as he removed a water bottle from his bag and handed it to me. I only stared at it before taking one from my bag. I wasn't ready to trust or forgive him that easily after what he had put me through. Not yet, anyway.

Animals and insects of the night sang around me, and I wished I could mute them all. I had to admit that I, too, was suddenly curious about where Xavier was taking us. I hadn't even bothered to ask before we left.

"I don't know. First things first. I'm getting us as far away from the pack as possible. We'll put a few cities between us and this place, and then find a town with no wolf packs and lay low."

Axel stepped around us, his hazel eyes shining oddly bright as he stared at the forest around us. "Okay. Well, I have a safe house, and no one else knows about it. It's about two days' drive from here, though. If we can make it there somehow, we can lay low more safely and take a little extra time to figure out our next move."

"Why do you have a safe house?" I asked as we started walking once more. Axel was now ahead of us and honestly, I didn't mind. I hadn't been comfortable with him walking behind me.

"All packs do. All *alphas* do. Wolves are very territorial, and not all packs are large. There has to be a place an alpha can go if he's challenged and he loses. That's if he survives the fight long enough to make it to their safe house. Don't you have one, too?"

I assumed that question was for Xavier, so I said nothing as I drank more water. This wasn't going to go well, I could tell. Nothing good could come from all three of us being together. They both hated each other.

"Yes, but all of those locations are known by at least two others. Olcan will no doubt have them checked out anyway."

"Well, fortunately, mine is completely off the grid. We'll need a car."

———— •◦ ◦•• ————

AXEL

A wolf walking almost three hours on a full moon isn't smart. By the time we made it off Blackmoon territory and found a road and a gas station, we were all exhausted and irritable. Well, I wouldn't say Xavier and I were exhausted. We were tired and definitely hungry, but Ruby was on an absolute warpath.

Neither of us had been able to speak to her until she had eaten three bags of snacks and drank the two coffees that I got at the gas station. Yes, I said *got* them there, not *bought* them there, since it was three in the morning and I had to break in.

Even with limitations of the full moon, Xavier and I had been clearly able to hear her crying in the bathroom. She came out with her face dry and her sassy attitude back to being less than appealing as if she hadn't just spent five minutes bawling her eyes out. I admired her for it, though. Our situation was one that would drive anyone crazy, and she was keeping it together better than I had expected.

It had been funny to see her standing there with a knife in her hands. I had no doubt in my mind that she wouldn't have hesitated to use it. It amazed me that she was ready to run headfirst into a fight with a werewolf, despite the obvious futility of such an action. The full moon wouldn't be enough to keep a werewolf male from incapacitating her, and she knew it. She as brave like a wolf, so I guess it made sense that she ended up mated to one... well, with her attitude, I guess it made sense she was mated to two of us.

Neither Xavier nor Ruby trusted me right now, and I couldn't really fault either of them for that. I wouldn't trust me either after the additional problems I've caused. I will always regret ever trusting that bastard Olcan. I should have known he had his own agenda. Killing Ruby or Xavier was never what I wanted.

I hope my beta had received my message and had taken my father away from the pack. While Mathieu's pack will be fine for now, Olcan might feel the need to get revenge on me and mine for me betraying him.

It was almost morning and the potions we drank would be wearing off in a few hours. Olcan will realize we're missing soon, if he hasn't already, and then we'll have people keeping an eye out for us. Or worse, rogue wolves. The faster we get out of here, the better. I looked up at the moon and buried my hands in my jacket pockets. This was going to be a journey and then some because neither of them trusted me or wanted me around. I wasn't in the mood to go out of my way to prove myself, but I'd have to work to gain their trust eventually or this would be much harder it needed to be. We had wasted precious minutes back there standing and bickering.

Also, while Ruby had been in the bathroom, Xavier had taken the time to warn me.

"I'm only okay with you being here because she needs to be protected, and I can't do it on my own if the Council decides to treat us like rogues."

"I think that's exactly what we are now, Xavier. But it's big of you to admit you can't care for her the way I can."

Of course, I knew that's not what he meant, but I hadn't been able to stop myself from razzing him just a bit. I hated how she stared at him as if he was the sun or moon and her world revolved around him. I hated how much she hung on to him as if he was keeping her grounded to the earth while she looked at me like I might steal her panties. I've treated her badly from the start, so I know I don't deserve her kindness. But dammit, I'm not a monster.

"You have nothing to worry about," I had told him to head off the inevitable argument. "Your girlfriend is yours and yours alone."

I closed my eyes and inhaled deeply. Why was I bothered about all of that anyway? I said it myself - I don't want to be with her - so why am I wasting brainpower obsessing about the connection she has with someone else? They were made for each other, and I was just unlucky enough to get tied into their romance. Maybe the goddess was punishing me by giving me a mate I can't really have

They were standing a few steps away from me bickering, and I honestly had no interest in listening to their conversation. We needed to find a car. I could smell rotting garbage, gas, and nature, and I frowned as I forced my senses to do better, to stretch further After a moment, I caught onto the scent I was looking for.

"There are humans near here," I said, and they looked my way as I removed my bag and placed it on the ground. "Maybe it's the owners for this place, but either way, I'm going to check if they have a car."

I started walking off when Ruby spoke. "Don't kill them."

I froze. I'm not used to words being hurtful because I rarely give a fuck about what people think of me, but that had stung. *So that's what she thinks of me? That I'm a cold-blooded killer?* I may hate humans, but I have never and would never kill them without reason. I shook my head and kept walking. "Don't worry, Ruby, I'll only kill them if they see me."

⚬⚫⚬

RUBY

Axel had been gone for twenty minutes before he returned with an SUV. It was a relief to get off my legs, but the awkward silence in the car was driving me up a wall.

I was sitting in the back while both men were in the front. I don't think either of them was particularly excited about being in such close proximity to each other. I looked from one man to the next, my annoyance peaking since neither made a move to turn the radio on. Did neither of them know that playing the radio is the number one way to cover an awkward silence? We'd been driving for almost an hour and no one had spoken since we had left the gas station.

I knew we were on the run for our safety, but at this point, I think Olcan's company would be preferable to these two brooding men. Olcan might be evil, but at least he was chatty. I hated awkward silences.

It was getting closer to dawn, and I desperately needed sleep. It had been a long night. No, a long couple of days and nights. I scooted closer to the door to rest my head against the window and sighed as I closed my eyes. They soon popped open after I started seeing more of those disturbing images behind them, the very things I didn't want to see more of.

No matter how exhausted I was, however, no matter how my legs felt like they were going to fall off, I couldn't sleep. I was haunted by the events that have happened so far, each and every time I closed my eyes. I kept seeing Olcan staring at me ,and I kept hearing screaming. Falling asleep would offer me a few minutes or hours of escape from this world, but now I wasn't even being afforded that basic luxury.

I tried to bring a good image to mind, the one of Xavier and me at the hidden falls. I focused on remembering the sound of the crashing water. I focused on the feel of it on my skin and tried to remember exactly how relaxed I had felt. After a while, my eyes closed and I must have fallen asleep because whispering voices had me jumping up. Thankfully, it wasn't the voices I had heard in the halls of Xavier's house. It was just Xavier and Axel talking.

I closed my eyes once more but tried to listen to what they were talking about. I soon gave up and moved forward so I was between them.

"What are you two talking about?" I asked as I looked from one to the next.

"Private conversation," Axel replied, and I flipped him the bird.

"Once we get to Axel's safe house, our next move has to be finding a way to break through that wall in your mind," Xavier replied. Axel, who was driving, nodded. "We'll just need to find a witch, a strong one."

"One that won't tell the entire supernatural community

about us," Axel added. "Witches gossip too much, and it'll be hard to find one that'll want anything to do with wolves, to begin with."

"What about Willow?" I suggested. She was the only witch I've met so far, and Xavier seemed to trust her. "If she's not strong enough to do it, maybe she'll know someone that is."

He nodded. "We'll see. You didn't sleep very long. How do you feel?"

"Like shit. I swear I'm usually more fit than this."

"I'll believe it when I see it." Axel murmured under his breath, and I pinned him with a glare. I was just about to give him a piece of my mind when Xavier leaned forward.

He looked from left to right on either side of the road, and soon Axel started to do the same. *Is this a wolf thing?* I wondered as I watched them when Xavier suddenly pinched his nostrils.

"What the fuck is that?" Xavier asked, and Axel's face twisted with disgust. I didn't smell anything however and it must be fuel with the way they both looked.

I inhaled deeply, but still, I didn't smell anything. "What? I don't smell anything."

"I can't explain it," Xavier said as he started to look in the back of the car, but there was nothing to see but our bags and me. "It's like something is rotting or dead, but there is another underlying smell as well. I feel like my eyes are going to start tearing up. What the hell is that?" The car suddenly swayed, and I was thrown against the door. "Axel, what the fuck?!"

"Something just ran across the road!" Axel yelled back, and the car suddenly accelerated. "Something's wrong here. Something is outside. That's what we smell."

"I've never smelled anything like this. What is it?"

Axel didn't respond. I leaned forward again, my hand holding onto Xavier's seat while the other massaged my shoulder that had smacked into the door. "Is it a supernatural?"

"With the incredible speed it ran across the road with, it must be. No human is that fast," Axel replied and his grip tightened on the steering wheel.

I couldn't see his face since I was behind him, but I could see his jaw and the way it was clenching. I looked over at Xavier, and he, too, looked more disturbed than I'd ever seen him. Then I remembered they still couldn't shift. They were vulnerable with some unknown supernatural creature following us.

"Maybe it's the Council. Maybe they sent someone, or something, after us," I said as I sat back. Axel was hitting 160mph, and I knew if he suddenly stepped on the break, I'd be thrown through the windscreen.

Axel shook his head, "They would have had to track our scent. The potions haven't worn off yet. Do you have a gun?"

Xavier nodded, "Yes. Ruby?"

I had grabbed for his bag as soon as he had said yes. As the lone human here, I wasn't happy knowing that there was something unknown out there that was threatening enough to rattle two male werewolves. For once in my life, just once, I'd like the universe to give me a win. And by a win, I mean a fucking break.

My hand touched something cold. I pulled the gun from the bag, but as I handed it to Xavier, something slammed into the car. I was thrown back against the door, my head slamming against the dark glass. Axel was cursing profusely as he tried to regain control of the car.

I didn't have time to see if my head was bleeding because I had to grip Xavier's seat with all my strength until the car stopped spinning. We swerved back and forth as Xavier dived into the back of the car to grab the gun that had fallen out of my hand and onto the seat.

Something barrelled into the car on the left side where I was, and I was thrown to the other side of the car as we were sent off the road.

"Xavier!" I screamed, but as soon as his name left my lips, the car came to a stop as it slammed into a tree.

I groaned and held my head, my hazy eyes trying to focus on the roof of the car that was still spinning. Whatever was outside was definitely trying to kill us. I sat up slowly, my hand holding the back of my head. Although I couldn't see anything, I could feel the warm liquid and knew I was bleeding.

I swallowed and blinked slowly, my eyes finally focusing when Axel appeared in the space between the seats, blood running down his face from a cut above his right brow.

"Ruby? Are you okay?" He asked me as he reached out to me. I pointed to Xavier, my hand shaking because there was a large crack in the windscreen where his head had hit it. He wasn't moving.

Axel grabbed him and pulled him back so he was sitting back in his seat and not hunched over the dashboard. He started to regain consciousness as he groaned and raised his hand to hold his head.

Neither of them was healing as quickly as I knew they could. "Xavier?" I called, my voice weak and broken, "It's still outside the car."

I shouldn't have said that. I never should have opened my mouth because a second later, Axel's door was ripped off the car. A clawed hand reached in and pulled him out.

I screamed. I screamed like I've never screamed before in my life as Axel's deep cry pierced through the night, and Xavier instantly regained full consciousness. He opened his car door shakily, and I did the same. I stumbled out, and strong hands grabbed me before I could fall onto my face.

This can't be happening. We've come so far; we had almost gotten away! Xavier started pulling me, but I was looking behind me for Axel. *We can't leave him, we can't just leave him.* The night had fallen silent once more, and my heart felt heavy with dread.

He can't be dead! Please don't let him be dead!

"Xavier!"

"Ruby, I need you to…"

He didn't finish his sentence as he was yanked away from me. I fell backward as I watched a man cloaked in darkness climb onto him. Xavier's howl pierced through the night as he fought the shadowy figure.

"Run!" Xavier yelled. "Ruby, run!"

I can't leave him! I can't I got to my feet, nonetheless, and started running. My eyes were blinded with tears, my body aching with pain, and my heart-breaking as I listened to Xavier's howls and cries. I pumped my legs despite the burning, but I didn't get far.

Something grabbed me and threw me forward. The pain burned through my left shoulder as I skidded on the cold highway. I tried to get up, but I only fell forward once more. I could hear slow footsteps behind me, and I rolled onto my back.

It wasn't a shadow. It was a man, but it was like no man I've ever seen. He was pale, his eyes like two flashlights in the dark, but what chilled me to my bone was when he opened his mouth and revealed his massive fangs.

I began dragging myself backward, the pebbles on the road cutting into my arms, but I couldn't stop. He was advancing on me, his lips pulling away into a wide smile.

"Please," I begged, my hot tears cooling as soon as they fell from my eyes to slide down my cheeks.

He tsk-tsked at me, and the last thing I saw as he fell onto me were his glowing red eyes. The last thing I felt was the piercing pain of fangs ripping into my throat.

THE STORY CONTINUES IN MY NEXT BOOK
LUNA CONFLICTED

RUBY

Have you ever been stabbed? Have you ever felt anything razor-sharp piercing into your body, tearing through skin and flesh? Do you have any idea how excruciating that is?

I could feel the man's pointed fangs slicing through my skin as if I was made of butter. I could feel his curved claws digging into my shoulders as he held me down to feed on me. I listened in abject horror as he slurped noisily on my blood.

So, this is how I die—being slurped on like a milkshake?

I screamed. My wide eyes that had been glued to the dark sky above in fright screwed tightly shut as I screamed for my life. I could feel my body growing weaker and weaker, the more he fed on me. My screams were muffled as he covered my mouth and forced my head to the side.

Xavier, Axel...are they dead?

Are they being fed on the way I am?

I could feel my tears sliding from my eyes. When I opened

them, I could barely see the world around me now as blurry as an impressionist painting. I could still feel the pain in my neck, but it felt almost distant. I was dying.

That was when it appeared—a shadow above the vampire. He was too busy feeding on me to notice it.

My eyelids felt like they were being weighed down by an anchor and though I tried, I couldn't call out to the shadow for help. I couldn't even move.

The vampire pressed down on my face and the world around me finally faded away.

I bolted upright, my hand gripping my chest as I gasped for breath. I started looking around me frantically, my eyes wide and my body shivering.

I was in a room, a dark room. For a second, I thought maybe it had all been a dream until my hand flew to my neck. My shoulders slumped as I felt the bandage there. Unfortunately, it had not been a dream, but instead a real-life nightmare.

Xavier. Axel.

The names echoed in my mind and I looked around the semi-dark room once more as I got out of the bed.

Where am I?

My only hope was that whoever saved me also saved Xavier and Axel as well. I had too many questions and no one to answer them. I decided to look for someone.

The hallway was dark, but I could see light down the hall coming from a room. The tiles were cold under my feet, my steps slow as I walked on my toes to prevent any sound of my approach. Whoever it was in that room might not be friendly. I still didn't know why that person saved me, or what their intentions were.

I stopped walking as I held onto the oversized shirt I was wearing. *Maybe it's the Council. Maybe they caught up with us just in time to save my life.* But if it was the Council that saved me, then my survival was merely temporary. After they got what they wanted from me, my life would still come to an end, just at their hands instead. *I need to find the guys. I hope they are alive to be found.* My chest tightened at the thought and I clenched my fists.

What was that man that bit me? I thought to myself as I continued walking. There had been just enough light for me to see his pale skin and crimson eyes. I still knew so little about the supernatural community, I could only guess that maybe he was a demon or a vampire. No, he couldn't have been. If Axel and Xavier couldn't tell what was hunting us by its scent, no way could he be a vampire. They would know what a demon or vampire smelled like, right?

From what I understood, werewolves used to act as protectors, assuming the role of watchdogs – no pun intended – for both the humans and the supernatural world alike. Now only some packs chose to function as guardians. Like Xavier's pack–they hunted down supernaturals who sought to create havoc or do harm. So wouldn't Xavier know any supernatural creature well enough by its scent?

Whispering voices met my ears as I drew closer to the door.

"We don't have a choice. We have to tell the others because they will be back. This will buy us time with the Council."

I felt a pang of relief as I made out Axel's voice, and then I frowned. Why was I so concerned for him? I rolled my eyes. I certainly was unhappy with his behavior towards me, but I didn't want anything serious to happen to him. Deep down, some part of me felt relieved he'd survived the attack.

"Once Ruby wakes up, we'll leave. Not before."

I closed my eyes and sighed as I heard Xavier speak. I walked into the room. Their gazes turned to me, but my eyes fell on a man standing to the left of the room.

His grey eyes found mine and he gave me a warm smile.

I returned it and looked away. "What's going on? What happened?"

Xavier walked over to me, his eyes glistening as he guided me to a chair. "Sit." He nodded almost imperceptibly at the grey-eyed man and then he backed away.

The stranger then moved to approach me, a strand of yellow blonde hair falling onto his forehead as he bent down.

I pulled away somewhat as the unknown man reached out to me.

He paused. "I'm only going to check your wound."

I looked at Xavier and then Axel, who had his arms crossed over his chest. I frowned because there was a thin pink line running from his left cheek down to his neck. No doubt, a wound he had suffered at the hands of the unknown supernatural that had already healed.

I exhaled and allowed the man to remove the bandage from my neck, wincing somewhat as the tape pulled at my skin.

He nodded as he stepped back. "All healed."

"Already?" Xavier asked, and Axel moved forward to see my neck. A look passed between them.

I reached up and touched the area. True enough, I was healed. The area felt completely smooth as if nothing had happened. I couldn't feel any evidence of the horrible trauma I endured, not even the raised skin of a telltale scar left behind. "Is there a mark?" I asked.

The man shook his head. "There is none," he replied as he glanced at Axel and then Xavier. He crossed the room to throw my bandage in a bin.

I watched him with narrowed eyes. *Who is he? Where the hell were we, anyway? How long had I been asleep in order for my wound to have healed completely? And how could I have healed without so much as a mark?* That man—creature had ripped into my throat.

I hadn't realized I had been slowly massaging the area until Xavier held my hand. It was as if I could still feel something there, despite being healed.

"How are you feeling?" he asked me, as he looked me up and down.

Suddenly aware that I was wearing nothing except a large T-shirt barely reaching my knees, my cheeks began to heat. "I feel fine." I pulled my hand away and interlocked my fingers on my lap. "I feel fine, just kind of in shock, I guess. What attacked us? How long have I been sleeping?"

Xavier sat down across from me while Axel remained standing, his hazel eyes piercing into me.

I still couldn't understand why I was so panicked when he'd been yanked out of the car. I'd felt a stab of fear so strong, I could barely think. I don't want to care about him, but apparently, that isn't completely under my conscious control. Some part of me did care about Axel, whether I wanted to or not. When had this happened? Would I have ever known how much I cared about Axel if we hadn't been placed in a life or death situation? How could I have feelings for a man who once almost yanked my hair out from the root as he dragged me out of his dungeon?

Maybe because he showed you he wasn't a complete asshole by leaving with you and Xavier, thereby putting himself and his pack at risk.

"You've been asleep for a good while," Axel replied, his gravelly voice carried through the room. He then pinched the bridge of his nose and turned away. "We were attacked by vampires."

So, I was right after all.

I studied Xavier thoughtfully, taking in his beautiful face. As his eyes hadn't left me since I walked into this room. I thought I had lost him when I heard him screaming as he'd faced the vampire while the pain in my heart had damn near killed me. I sighed. "Why did neither of you know that it was vampires outside the car when you first smelled them?" My eyes drifted to Axel when he turned around to stare at me. "You two panicked."

"I didn't panic," Axel retorted.

I made a face. *Who is he kidding?* "Yes, you did. I was there...remember? Why don't you guys know what vampires smell like?" I stared at Xavier, whose lips formed a thin line, and

I frowned. The room was filled with silence and my eyes found the blonde man who'd been listening to our conversation quietly.

He was holding his chin, a finger gliding back and forth over his lips.

No one seemed interested in answering me.

Axel dug his hands into his pockets.

Xavier's soothing voice licked at my ears, "This is the first time either of us has met a vampire."

Axel cleared his throat. "Vampires have been extinct for hundreds of years."

I frowned as I tilted my head to the side. "What?" The blonde man briefly drew my attention as he left the room, then I glanced back over at Axel. He'd certainly piqued my interest with that unexpected statement. *So, if vampires had been extinct for hundreds of years, how exactly had one just ripped into my throat?*

Axel sat down and crossed his legs.

I noticed for the first time just how exhausted both Xavier and he looked.

"What we know about vamps now comes from stories told to us over the years," Xavier said. "They were said to be bloodthirsty and animalistic, with no shred of thought other than the drive to quench their ravenous thirst."

Axel sat forward, his elbows on his knees. The strands of his hair loose from his bun slid forward to cover his cheeks. "Vampires were the parasites of the earth. Their only purpose was to exist, feed, and populate."

An image of the vampire that attacked me appeared in my mind as Axel spoke and a chill passed through my body.

"Their thirst for blood, any and every creature's blood, is insatiable," Axel went on. "As a result, they lived as outcasts. They belonged to no community, supernatural or otherwise, because they contaminated and killed everything they came into contact with. Years ago, werewolves, humans, and several other supernaturals banded together and waged war on them, wiping them out for good."

"Umm, I think they survived," I replied under my breath.

"Clearly." Axel nodded. "They were said to be pale, hideous creatures capable of turning any living being–human, werewolf, witch, anyone–into bloodsuckers like themselves. Their venom is so strong, it is capable of completely changing one's anatomy–completely erasing who and what you are. They were among the most dangerous supernatural beings in existence." He shook his head. "Still are, apparently."

I nodded.

Xavier ran his hand down his face, pulling his cheeks down. "I can't figure out how they've survived without anyone knowing. In all the stories I've heard, no one ever mentioned that their scent is so strong. How have they masked it for so many years?"

That vampire that attacked me had indeed been pale, but he hadn't been hideous. Maybe he hadn't shown his true self? He also hadn't seemed like a bloodthirsty, thoughtless creature. Well, bloodthirsty, maybe. But thoughtless? No, I'd gotten the feeling he'd been a lot closer to a human or werewolf in thoughts and motivations than Axel and Xavier's stories were depicting. "So, what are we going to do?" I asked as I looked at them both.

"We have no choice but to go back home," Xavier replied as he tapped a finger on the arm of the chair.

"No," I said as I shook my head. "I can't go back. The two of you know I can't. Vampires or not, the Council wants me dead. Have you both forgotten that?"

Axel huffed. "Forgotten it? It's the reason we left. It's the reason we were attacked by vampires. How can we forget, Ruby? You need to remember that they want Xavier and me dead as well now. This isn't only about you."

"Axel," Xavier said in a warning tone.

I bit my lip and looked away. Axel was right. My life wasn't the only one on the line here, but I was scared. Not only was I running from the all-powerful werewolf Council, but now there were vampires on the loose out there, ones that even intimidated two full-grown male werewolves.

These two men were alphas-to-be. In fact, Axel was an alpha in all but name. Yet, they had their asses handed to them when they'd faced off against that vamp. Sure, it had been a full moon, and they had been caught off guard. But still, I did feel terrified of anything that could strike fear into these two men. I didn't know about the guys, but I wasn't interested in becoming some vampire's lunch, or worse, getting turned into a vamp myself.

"Ruby?"

I looked Xavier's way as my name glided off his lips like honey.

"This new threat, it's very serious," he said. "If vampires are back and we know they are, this means trouble. We have to warn my dad and the Council. Other packs need to know this. I don't know much about vampires, but if the stories are true, then the entire world is in danger."

"The stories are true," Axel added. "Even if they have been altered over time, the danger vampires pose is real. They are savages, and because of their infectious bite, they multiply quickly. We don't know how many people were turned before we were attacked."

I wanted to ask him why we couldn't simply call Mathieu and warn him, but I knew that would be selfish. I'd been lucky to survive being bitten...I knew this. If vampires decided to attack now, how many more would die if they maintained their element of surprise? "Okay," I replied as I scratched at my brow and closed my eyes. I quickly reopened them when I started to get a flashback of the vampire as he attacked me, his glistening white fangs aimed directly at my throat. "Okay," I repeated, as I rolled my shoulders and sat up straight. "We do need to warn everyone."

Axel sat back and reclined in his seat, his eyes lowering into slits. "There's a book that has been in my family for generations. Supposedly, it holds the history of werewolves and other supernatural beings. I was never allowed to look inside it as a child. In fact, it's been so long since I've even seen it that I'd almost forgotten about it." He looked back and forth between the two of us, a contemplative look on his face. "It contains information on vampires, their weaknesses, and how to fight them. Any knowledge we can gain from it about vampires will be helpful since we know so little right now."

At this point, I was barely listening to him. My mind had taken me back to that highway, to the moment when I felt my blood gushing from my neck as that vampire consumed it. My shoulder twitched, something like a phantom feeling still present there.

"Ruby?" Xavier called to me.

My head snapped towards him.

He stared at me with concern.

I looked away, my eyes downcast to the floor. "I thought I was going to die," I said under my breath. "I thought you were both dead."

"We almost were," Axel replied.

I watched him from under my lashes.

He looked angry, and I could understand why. He wasn't someone that liked feeling out of control—this much I knew. He got his ass kicked and I could only imagine the level of his rage right now. The severity of the cut on his face underscored just how close of a call it had been.

"Who was he?" I asked. "The shadow. You know the person that saved us? Did either of you see him?" I lowered my voice. "Was it blondie?"

Axel frowned as he rose to stretch.

The action struck me as odd. It seemed too mundane coming from Axel. I supposed he must be tired. He certainly looked tired, anyways. Why did it seem as if neither Xavier nor he had rested the way I had? I glanced over at Xavier.

He'd been propping his head up with his hand, his eyes staring ahead. He appeared lost in thought.

I realized he'd barely spoken. "How long have we been here?"

His eyes shifted to me. "We've been here for two days."

"Blondie, as you called him," Axel interjected. "Wasn't the one that saved us. We're at my safe house right now, and he's the warlock I hired to watch the place. He keeps the place protected with warding. Whoever saved us and killed those vamps, got us here in a matter of hours."

I frowned as my eyes widened.

"He said there was a knock at the door and when he opened it, we were lying on the ground outside." Axel pointed at my neck. "Your wound was already almost healed and only bleeding a little. The same goes for us and our wounds. I, for one, feel drained. That fucker almost drained me."

I understood now, that's why they looked so beaten.

"On the other hand, you seem to have recovered rather quickly, especially for a human," Axel continued as he studied me suspiciously. "A little warlock magic was needed, but I would have expected your wounds to have healed slower. Your blood count would certainly take some additional time to replenish."

My eyes narrowed at his tone and the way he was staring at me. I shrugged, not sure what to say to him. How was I to answer that? "Considering this was my first time having my neck ripped open by a vampire, I don't know what to tell you. We can compare how fast I heal if it ever happens again."

And just like that, my anger at Axel returned.

"Whoever saved us must have done something to save Ruby first," Xavier said. "We were almost beyond the point of no return. It would have taken less effort to drain Ruby, I would assume, given her smaller size in comparison to us. Either way, I think it's clear that at least someone out there knows about these vamps and how to kill them. Were they just in the right place at the right time, or did they already know what was going to happen? And how did they know where to take us if this safe house is unknown to others, even Axel's pack?" He questioned, looking at Axel as he said it.

Then Xavier stood and ran his hand down his shirt. "There are a lot of questions about how we survived. All we really know is that we did. But right now, getting back to the pack has to be our priority." He turned to leave the room and paused. "Come on," he said to me. "You need to eat."

My stomach chose that moment to growl.

Want to know what happens next in this series?
Read Luna Conflicted

LUNA RISING WORLD

<hr>

LUNA RISING SERIES

Luna Rising

Luna Captured

Luna Conflicted

Luna Darkness

Luna Chosen

<hr>

Want to know what happened before Luna Rising?
Read Bloodmoon Wars Series!

<hr>

BLOODMOON WARS SERIES

The Awakening

The Enlightenment

The Revolution

The Renaissance

The New Age

Ever wonder what happens after a wolf dies?

Read Wolf Reborn series to find out!

THE WOLF REBORN SERIES

Wolf Reborn

Wolf Burdened

Wolf Scorned

Wolf Fallen

Wolf Embraced

OTHER SERIES BY SARA SNOW

DESTINE ACADEMY

Destine Academy - The Complete Series

CURSED MATES SERIES

Cursed Mates

Cursed Pack

Cursed Storm

Cursed Rage
Cursed Fates

———•◦ ◦•———

GEMINI WOLVES

Moon Pledged

Moon Touched

Moon Promised

———•◦ ◦•———

SHATTERED KINGDOM

Shattered Kingdom

Stolen Kingdom

Ruined Kingdom

———•◦ ◦•———

VENANDI CHRONICLES

Demon Marked

Demon Kissed

Demon Huntress

Demon Desire

Demon Eternal

———•◦ ◦•———

THE FALLEN BLOOD SERIES

Dark Mate

Fallen Mate

Runaway Mate

Replaced Mate

Broken Mate

Eternal Mate